BRINK

A Novel

Dan Chakonas

Cover design by Dan Chakonas
Cover background photo licensed from Big Stock Photo

Please visit Solitude Books on the web to order, and to discover exciting future titles!

www.solitudebooks.com

Copyright © 2012 Dan Chakonas
All rights reserved.
ISBN: 0615730345
ISBN-13: 978-0615730349 (Solitude Books)

For my Papou, with whom I am proud to share a name

"Death is not the worst
that can happen to men."

Plato
427 BC – 347 BC

PROLOGUE

Being beaten by three men while handcuffed to a chair in a disgusting interrogation room would make anyone angry, but Aldo Brink seethed with rage for a different reason. At 37, Brink possessed more operational experience than men twenty years his senior, and had it been up to him, this wouldn't have happened. He had never been captured before and this time it was only because someone tipped off the targets about his team's arrival. They were picked up by corrupt local authorities almost immediately upon arriving in Bolivia. Their false identities, known only to a handful of people back home, had been provided to their captors. They never stood a chance.

When picked up just outside their rented apartment, Brink had entertained thoughts of fighting it out on the street and going down guns blazing. They were outnumbered twenty to one at least, but he had mentally prepared for death years ago, and he had conquered those odds before. Death did not scare him in the slightest. He preferred a quick death by a bullet to the head as opposed to months of agonizing torture, but when he saw the two other men who accompanied him get taken into custody he thought it was selfish to choose a quick death in a gunfight while letting them rot away in a torture chamber alone. No, if they were going to die, they would do it together and suffer equally.

Brink could hear the screams of his friends, Rodney and Hakim Harrison from the room down the hall. They were brothers from Atlanta, Georgia, separated by a mere two years. He had never known anyone as tough as the Harrison brothers and assumed it came from their upbringing as Army brats who eventually followed in their father's footsteps.

Just by looking, you could instantly tell they were brothers. They were both built like brick walls, but Hakim was the burlier of the two at 6'6, 285. Rodney was an inch shorter and about forty pounds lighter. Hakim had played defensive end at Army and even received some interest by a few professional teams. While playing pro ball was almost every college guy's dream, Hakim had decided long ago to follow his older brother Rodney into the Army.

Their black skin and imposing stature made them stand out among their group of operators. The entire Black Ops roster of field agents inside the no name unit of the CIA was never more than twelve people at any given time. All were white, with the exception of the Harrison brothers. Hakim, the jokester of the two, often reminded his brother and Brink that they were the "blackest black ops" members. Rodney would roll his eyes every time his little brother said the line. Unlike Hakim, he gave no quarter to humor, or any type of foolishness for that matter.

Aldo Brink had Italian roots, and that completed the knowledge he had about his family. While the Harrison brothers hailed from the South, Brink was born and raised in California. He had been abandoned at an orphanage run by Italian American Catholic Nuns who found him on their doorstep with a note that said his name. He grew up there and joined the Army when he turned 18.

Brink had no one, but Rodney and Hakim had a strong family. Their father had a long honorable military career, and earned a Silver Star in Korea. Their mother made sure they said their prayers before every meal and before going to bed. Brink never knew his parents, but somehow he knew they were nothing like Mr. and Mrs. Harrison, so maybe he was better off, he thought.

While their backgrounds couldn't have been more different, they became fast friends after their first operation together years ago. Brink had far more experience, but he found the Harrison brothers to be the best wingmen any operator could ask for.

The three of them worked for the most covert unit of the CIA. Even novices were familiar with the CIA's clandestine service, but they belonged to something else entirely. The clandestine service was staffed with dedicated people of all backgrounds who served their country with honor to be sure, but something more flexible, efficient, and ruthless was needed. That is where Brink and the Harrison brothers came in.

They reported to the Director of the CIA, and to his deputy. The unit didn't even have a name and currently consisted of only six field agents, and a small support staff. Fewer than 20 people knew of their existence. If anything went wrong, they would be disavowed.

Today, something had gone very wrong. There would be no rescue, and no acknowledgement of all they had done to protect America over the years.

Before his captors hurled him into the interrogation room, his blindfold had fallen off just enough for Brink to see that there were a total of two rooms connected by a long hallway. The screams he heard gave away their positions, so he knew Rodney and Hakim were in the room right down the hall next to him. They were probably trying to get one brother to talk by threatening the other one, Brink thought. *Hold on, guys.*

"You will talk to me! Do you want me to use this?" His captor stroked the large bowie knife that for now remained sheathed on his belt.

Brink had already formulated a plan. He sized up his opposition quickly. They were nasty characters, but not professionals. They were waiting for their boss, and Brink's target, Alejandro Alvarez. Until he got there, Brink would be roughed up. After he got there, it would be…worse.

Alvarez was 45, a former paratrooper, and a Bolivian political leader on the rise. He also held the infamous distinction of being responsible for the deaths of 73

Americans, including two U.S. Senators when he bombed a commercial flight traveling from Brazil to Florida. He was as dangerous a terrorist as anyone in the Middle East, but your average citizen had never heard of him due to nonexistent media coverage. That is, until the day a flight blew up off the Florida coast.

Brink and his team traveled to Bolivia, and planned to kill Alvarez. Being burned by someone back home wasn't part of the plan. Who did and why was a matter Brink would deal with, but obviously there were more pressing matters needing attention first.

The foot soldiers who cuffed him to the chair had frisked him, but missed the lock pick hidden inside the fabric behind the belt loops of his pants. *Amateurs.*

Brink had picked the lock on his handcuffs a good two minutes ago, but still sat there taking punches. He only had one shot, and he wouldn't waste it by acting prematurely.

He braced himself for another punch as it landed squarely across his face. He spit some blood onto the floor as one of the foot soldiers moved closer and growled with a bit too much bravado for the other two terrorists in the room, who rolled their eyes at their overzealous comrade.

As the idiot continued his false bravado, a muffled voice emerged from his hand radio that Brink assumed came from the guard outside.

"He's coming in."

That's what Brink needed to hear. The second his captor turned his back to reply through his radio, Brink rose from his chair and pulled the knife he had been threatened with from his captor's sheath. The knife sliced the man's throat before he even realized it had been taken from him.

As the man clutched his neck trying hopelessly to stop the blood from pouring out of it, Brink pushed him forward into another one of his captors, giving him just enough time to wheel right and throw the knife into the forehead of the third guard who stood by the door. Brink sprinted towards the last man who had shed his dying friend, but now found himself covered in blood, and a bit disoriented. *Amateurs.*

Brink reached him just as the man drew his gun, and readied to fire. He grabbed him by the wrist and pushed sideways moving the gun into a safe position where if it went off, only the cement wall would suffer. After getting up close, Aldo Brink's years of Muay Thai training took over.

Pulling the man's head down and unleashing a series of quick knee strikes into the man's ribs had him gasping for breath. As he hunched over in agony, one final knee to the bridge of the nose knocked him out cold. The man collapsed toward the ground. Brink caught him by the throat before he hit the floor. Breaking his neck took only a few seconds.

After wiping the blood off the knife on the shirt of the deceased, he grabbed two pistols off the floor, checked their ammo, and racked their slides. He quietly opened the door and moved down the hall.

Brink took a deep breath, inhaling the musty air, just before he burst through the door with his pistol raised. Spotting only two guards, he fired two shots with speed and precision. Both men fell instantly.

Rodney and Hakim were strung up by a rope and pulley system attached to the ceiling with their arms raised above their heads. Besides two bruised faces, they looked as good as possible given the circumstances. Once he cut Rodney free, the elder brother moved to the door as the lookout while Brink cut Hakim down. Brink tossed one of the pistols to Rodney. Hakim picked up another off the dead guard that had pistol whipped him moments earlier.

A foot solider emerged from around the corner, coming face to face with Rodney. The elder brother wasted no time and grabbed the man by his neck and hurled him back towards his younger brother. Hakim unleashed a right cross that caved in the terrorist's face. He knocked the man out cold and probably caused him brain damage, Brink thought. *Thank God I don't have to take one of his punches.*

It turned out it wasn't just a regular foot soldier that Hakim Harrison had obliterated with one punch. It had been one of Alejandro Alvarez's bodyguards. Brink knew this because standing right in front of him in the hallway that was supposed to lead to his team's death stood the man himself. The man they were sent to kill stood not ten feet from them, frozen in fear.

Brink wanted to capture him, or take him into the room they were just in and torture him for information about how their mission had been compromised, but he knew they had no time for that. They had to get out of there now before the cavalry of radicals and corrupt local police arrived.

Brink raised his pistol and fired, putting one between his eyes. Alvarez's lifeless body hit the disgusting floor just as Brink and the Harrison brothers arrived at the end of the hall, rounded the corner, and reached daylight.

As he saw his friends disappear into a sea of people in the crowded street market, he knew they would be fine. They were smart, had some serious equipment stashed away that they could barter with, and had some contacts that could help them while keeping things discreet. They would stay in touch, but it would never be the same. Brink couldn't help but think they were right.

The Harrison brothers had decided that enough was enough. They were done. They weren't going back home, and tried their best to convince their buddy, Aldo Brink, to join them. This was the last straw of not being able to trust their own government that sent them around the world.

Maybe they were right, Brink thought. Maybe the time had come to disappear and get the Hell out while he still could. But who else would do what he did? Innocent Americans needed him out there even if they didn't know it. Brink had begun to have these internal debates with himself for a while, but blocked them out for the sake of his own sanity.

He selfishly wanted them to stay with him. Among the group with no name, they were the ones he trusted with his life without question. In their line of work, that level of trust was hard to achieve. He promised Rodney and Hakim he would tell their superiors they died while trying to escape. He would say he saw their bodies and would guarantee they were dead. That would keep the heat off. With Brink testifying to their valiant escape attempt, no one would think twice about it, and no one would look for them. When he got back to DC, Brink would make good on his promise.

Now, he looked forward to getting home. Once back and settled, he would try to find out what went wrong, but he had something of a totally different nature on his mind now. For the first time in almost a week he felt a smile start to emerge. He had an appointment to keep for something that he hadn't done in years.

Aldo Brink had a date.

CHAPTER 1

The most important day of Aldo Brink's life had arrived. Today marked the two year anniversary of his first date with Jazlyn Reyes and the day he would propose to her. He wasn't the type to wax poetic about his great luck, but in this case he couldn't help it.

She worked at the prestigious think tank the Energy Security Center for Policy or ESCP and possessed expertise in the field of energy development with a focus on international relations. She had testified before Congress multiple times and had been asked for off the record advice on the subject by members of both political parties.

Brink had seen over the years just how intelligent and accomplished she was and he respected the Hell out of her for it. He didn't give praise easily, but she deserved all her success and then some, he thought.

While her mind had deepened his love for her over the past two years, he confessed that her gorgeous pair of legs were the first thing that caught his eye. He recalled their fated meeting at a black tie fundraiser they both attended for wounded veterans hosted by the ESCP.

The large ballroom overflowed with power players. Everywhere you looked, members of Congress, military brass, Fortune 500 CEO's, Wall Street tycoons, and oil barons jockeyed for position among the well-heeled crowd. Brink had been invited by the top organizer of the event with whom he had bunked with in Army basic training years ago. Though not one for parties, he would have felt bad turning down such a gracious offer. It was for a good cause after all and from the day he began his covert training up until today his social life had all but disappeared. As hard a man as he was, Brink knew he still needed some normal human contact outside of his work relationships. He thought this fundraiser party fit the bill.

Brink actually felt good in his tuxedo. It was something different and quite the change of pace for him, so perhaps that explained it, he thought. It had been over a year since he wore it. The last time he donned this particular garment he had travelled undercover to Rome as a high-end art connoisseur tracking some particularly nasty people. By the time the operation ended, the tux needed a good cleaning while he needed someone to pull a .38 slug out of his shoulder. He always said, sometimes evil wears a suit.

After only an hour there, he wanted to leave. He had made the requisite small talk and been a gentleman when an older woman asked him for a dance. Brink wasn't about to say no to a dance with a senior citizen who had been a nurse during WWII. Sixty years ago she could have been that woman in that famous picture kissing a G.I. in the street when the war ended, Brink thought. When the dance ended, he gave her a courtly kiss on the cheek and complimented her attire, as well as her moves.

"You're just adorable, you made this old woman feel young again," she said.

"My pleasure, I am sure you were quite the heartbreaker."

Brink bid her farewell and started to move to the door when someone caught his eye. At the bar on a stool, wearing an elegant black dress with a high slit up the side that revealed a perfect pair of long athletic legs, sat a woman of stunning beauty. With her legs seductively crossed, and with an exotic face that only had a hint of makeup on it, she had him transfixed. He could sense her strength and confidence from across the room. Brink eyeballed her all the way from her flowing black hair down to her dangerous looking Jimmy Choo heels. *Who the Hell is that?*

Jazlyn Reyes recently turned a fit looking 33, and felt happy to be at the event. She believed in raising money for veterans as much as anyone, but she had grown tired of the slimy big shots trying to put the moves on her. Like Brink, she did not suffer fools well. Had she been at a local bar she would have told off the men currently hitting on her. They were getting increasingly belligerent as their alcohol intake increased, but she wanted to maintain a professional demeanor since she was there representing the ESCP. Even so, her patience had worn thin, especially since the man nearest to her reeked, from more than alcohol.

She found herself mere seconds away from unleashing a barrage of curse words in Spanish at her over aggressive pursuers, when a handsome man appeared and gently took her hand. While not encroaching on her personal space, Aldo Brink lightly touched her hand, and looked right into her eyes.

"My dear, you look so unhappy, and I can't stand to be around unhappy people, so I felt I had to intervene. Would you care to dance?"

"I'd love to," she replied.

Brink gently led her to the crowded dance floor, put one hand behind her back, and lightly pulled her in close. She stood tall, Brink noticed. She wore heels which made her almost as tall as he was. At 6'1, that meant she stood 5'8 or 5'9 without them, he guessed. As he stared into her dark brown eyes, he secretly hoped she wasn't one of the many politicians in attendance after all the nasty, yet true things he had said about them over the years. As an operator he possessed the skill to blend in, but in his real life subtlety wasn't his forte.

"I saw you over there surrounded by the hyenas, and I thought to myself, this lovely woman needs a dance," Brink said as they moved slowly with the music.

"You see a lot."

"Always."

"I spotted you checking me out before you came over." *Busted.*

"I plead no contest, but could you blame me? You look absolutely stunning."

"Lawyer?" she asked.

Aldo Brink and the legal profession were about as far apart as the Earth and Pluto.

"Do I look that unethical?" he asked as he spun her around and pulled her back in close.

"I think you look just *fine*."

He smiled. "Aldo Brink, international security analyst extraordinaire."

"Jazlyn Reyes. I never thought I would meet a man with a first name more interesting than mine."

Her dance partner's strong hands and dark mysterious features did not go unnoticed as she surveyed every inch of him that she could with her hands and perfectly manicured nails.

As they danced she told him where she worked and why she attended the fundraiser. She explained how her parents came to America from Brazil when she was 7, how she studied geology and energy development, and how she had risen to become one of the top fellows at the ESCP. She turned out to be extremely well traveled, spoke Portuguese and Spanish fluently, and had been to just about every country on Earth where significant energy potential existed.

The music seemed to go on forever but neither of them seemed to mind. Brink wanted to ask her out to dinner, but he had to leave for Bolivia tomorrow and wouldn't be back for a few days, assuming he returned in one piece.

Her forthrightness ultimately rendered his hesitation moot.

"Aldo Brink, we should go out to dinner tomorrow."

"I would love to, but I leave tomorrow on a business trip and won't be returning until the end of the week," he said with genuine regret in his voice.

"In that case, you call me and we will make plans. Cell number is on there," she said, as she reached into her incredibly small handbag and handed him her business card just as the song ended.

"You will be hearing from me. I promise."

"OK, but since you're making me wait for dinner, I insist on one more dance," she playfully demanded.

The music started once again and Brink brought her hand up to his lips and kissed it. "Of course," he said.

As a smart man, Brink knew the implications of having any kind of relationship outside of work, given the life he led. He could never tell her everything and would have to lie to her in order to protect her, his colleagues, the country, and himself. As always, he thought far ahead. This great skill kept him alive, after all. Sometimes though, you just had to live for the moment. This was one of those times.

They danced for a minute in silence as she rested her head on his shoulder before speaking again.

"Ever been to Rome? I just love that city," she inquired.

"Well, now that you mention it…"

CHAPTER 2

Aldo Brink sprinted up the street, just as he finished his morning run up and down the Potomac River. As he rounded the corner of the winding scenic road, his home came into view. Having been designed by an architect who lived in it until moving to the West Coast, it was considerably more contemporary in appearance than most of the homes in the area. It had two bedrooms, two and a half baths, an office, and a narrow but long pool a few steps from the back door that Brink swam laps in whenever he could. Situated in a wooded and hilly area, it had a great view of the Potomac. He purchased it a little over a year ago, trading up from his rented studio near downtown.

Brink worked so often that he rarely had any time to spend his salary. His modest income, saved and invested over the years, had turned into quite a nest egg. Still, the house taunted him with its unaffordable price. He got lucky when the architect decided to retire and move to California.

The house was priced to sell fast. When he heard Brink served in the Army, he took an additional twenty thousand off the price. He had been an Army Captain in Korea before he studied architecture. Brink bought it and thanked the man for his generosity. "If we don't look out for each other, nobody will," the architect said.

Brink sat on the front steps of his unique residence taking in the fresh spring morning air when he heard a dreadful sound. He had left his encrypted smartphone inside, but he could hear it ringing through an open window. The ringtone told him the call came from work. Brink obeyed a standing order that his phone must be within an arm's length at all times, no matter what. The one exception to this rule was if the Director or Deputy Director of the CIA authorized him to go off the grid in order to clear his head or just take some time off. The job's stressful nature meant some time off here and there served an essential function for operators to recharge both mentally and physically.

Today was one of those days. He had been granted a two day respite after asking for some personal time. Only Brink knew that he planned to use this time to propose to Jazlyn Reyes, his girlfriend of two years. The fact that his phone rang meant something very important must be going on. Brink gave them his body, heart, and soul, and all he asked for in return was to be left alone during his minimal vacation time. His superiors had always respected this unwritten code, until now.

Brink took his time going up the steps and took one final breath of the fresh morning air before stepping inside and snatching his smartphone from the breakfast table where he left it. For a split second he thought about hitting ignore, but thought better of it and answered without looking at the caller ID.

"I don't care who this is, and if you think I'm coming in to the office today, I'm hanging up right now. So, what can I do for you?"

"It's Sam, and a good morning to you too." Sam Hodges served as Deputy Director of the CIA and usually operated as the man Brink reported to. To say they had a contentious relationship would be an understatement. "The ladies men want to talk to you in person."

"You're kidding."

"I'm afraid not."

Aldo Brink took a deep breath, and wished he had ignored the call. The "ladies men" referred to the President and Vice President. What their nicknames lacked in respect, they made up for in accuracy. "OK, when?"

"Noon sharp, White House. Shouldn't take too long since they have a lunch engagement soon after."

"Fine, but just so you know after this meeting I'm not coming back to work until the day after tomorrow, so whatever you people are cooking up, take that fact into account."

After hanging up with Sam, Brink took a long shower. He put his head down and let the hot water calm his nerves. The lean muscular body he possessed had all the signs of almost two decades worth of war. Scars, burns, bullet holes, and knife wounds were his autobiography. His body held more evidence of his career than any file folder at the office. Because he often worked outside the law, only a slim paper trail existed about him. The vast majority of the records about what he had done resided in the heads of a few key people, while some others had bits and pieces.

As far as most people knew, he worked as a security analyst who had an office at CIA headquarters in Langley. He worked as a run of the mill employee, just like thousands of others.

He never talked about the details of his work with Jazlyn, and she understood why. He told her the scars were from his Special Forces A-Team days and she believed him, to a point. One intimate night she noticed a new wound that couldn't have happened at the office or on the basketball court. She told him that over time she had begun to suspect that he did more than just analyze for the CIA, and that she understood. She kissed him, and that was that. She trusted him and didn't need to know any more. Jazlyn knew him to be one of the good guys in every sense of the word, and that was good enough for her.

After his shower, Brink brushed his teeth and used some cool mint mouthwash. He combed his thick, curly, jet black hair straight back, keeping it short and simple as always. He emerged minutes later from the small walk-in closet dressed in a grey two button suit, white dress shirt, and black leather shoes that in a pinch he could sprint in without difficulty. He never wore a tie with this suit, and White House or not, today would be no different.

His only other suit, a black one, hung in the closet still in its dry cleaning plastic bag. Brink had picked it up last night on the way home. A perfectly clean suit was a must for when he proposed to Jazlyn. Normally, he would wear a dark suit with a tie when he went to the White House where he had been several times over the years, but if he did, he wouldn't have time to get it dry cleaned again before the evening he had planned with her. It was his day off anyway, and if anyone gave him shit about not wearing a tie, he would tell them where to get off.

He poured himself a small glass of orange juice and toasted an English muffin as he flicked through some news stories on his tablet computer. After breakfast, he washed his hands and headed to the bedroom. There, he opened the cabinet in his bedside nightstand, and punched the four digit code into the safe. When the lock sprung open he exchanged the smaller Glock 26 that he had holstered inside his waistband during his morning run with the larger Glock 17 in its holster inside the safe. After locking the smaller pistol in the safe, he placed the Glock on his right hip. A magazine pouch with two spare 17 round magazines was then placed on his left side.

Brink had an incredible amount of experience with every firearm you could imagine, but wasn't married to any of them. Whichever tool he needed to get the job done, he would use. For just walking around, when technically off duty, he had no problem trusting his Generation 4 Glock

17 9mm and its mini counterpart the Glock 26 when he took a run. They were tough and reliable. Just like him, he thought.

If for some reason he ever got stopped by the police, carrying a concealed firearm would cause a problem if not for the special identification he carried that identified him as a federal security officer authorized to carry one. The officer would simply call in and verify the information and Brink would be on his way. It had never happened before, but it was good to have just in case. He double checked the magazine, tapped his inside jacket pocket for his wallet, and then headed for the garage, grabbing his keys off the dresser as he left.

His place had a two car garage, but he only needed one of the spaces. The empty spot became useful when Jazlyn came over, but most of the time he pulled his Jerez Black BMW M3 right into the middle of the garage. He bought it for two reasons just after he moved into his new house. The first was that he loved it. The second, he never let Jazlyn know, but he wanted to pick her up for dates in a nice car, and not in his old Ford. It seemed a bit juvenile, and he knew it. Jazlyn would ride in a car straight from the junkyard as long as Aldo Brink sat behind the wheel.

The 414 horsepower engine went to waste on this trip. Traffic piled up a bit heavier than usual, so he slogged his way for about thirty minutes to a parking garage on G Street, a mere two blocks from the White House. Brink's license plate resided on file with the Capitol Police as well as the police departments of all the surrounding states. The file instructed all law enforcement to never stop or ticket the vehicle for any reason. On a few occasions, Brink had the need to quickly run people down around Washington and being harassed by local enforcement would have made it impossible. While tempting, Brink never abused this privilege and always drove safely and within the law unless national security or lives were at stake.

After paying the outrageous fee to park, he walked a short way to the southwest appointment gate of the White House. He checked in with the uniformed Secret Service agent, and handed over his credentials. The agent took notice of his ID's and ability to carry a firearm.

"Sir, are you currently carrying a firearm or weapon of any kind?" the agent asked.

"No. I know the Secret Service policy on that. Only the Secret Service is allowed weapons inside the perimeter." Brink left his Glock in the car back at the parking garage for this very reason. He could have checked his gun at the gate, but Brink knew he wouldn't know the agent working the gate, and no one touched his weapons unless he personally knew them.

"Thank you, sir. Please give me a moment as I call in your appointment to verify." The agent made the call and afterwards motioned Brink to proceed. He breezed through the metal detector and when no alert sounded he was led by another man up West Executive Ave. to just outside the West Wing where the head of the President's protection detail, Chris Spencer, stood waiting.

"Oh my God, who let you in here?"

"I dug a tunnel," Brink said.

Spencer was an older guy, strong as an ox, and had protected four Presidents. He fell into a small category of the twenty or so people who knew Aldo Brink, and his capabilities. They became close friends after Brink saved the previous President from certain death. He had unearthed a serious plot and tried to warn the Secret Service, but bureaucratic bullshit among the CIA, FBI, and Secret Service held up the information from getting to Spencer in time. Brink showed up in the nick of time and the whole incident was classified. The news that evening made mention of a minor disturbance at a fundraiser the President attended and that the Commander in Chief was never in any danger. *Bullshit.*

In truth, the President came within minutes of being killed and without the illegal methods of CIA black ops agent Aldo Brink, Chris Spencer would have gone down in history as the agent in charge who lost a President, even though vital information had been kept from him due to other people's incompetence. The two men never spoke of the incident, but Spencer always felt he owed him one to say the least.

Spencer put his old friend in a bear hug and lifted him off the ground. Brink took it all in good fun. "When I was told you were coming, I made sure I was here to greet you."

"It's always great to see you."

"Director Abraham just arrived."

Brink felt surprised. He wasn't told that the director of the CIA Donald Abraham would be there. "I was told the ladies men wanted to see me. That's all I know," Brink said.

Spencer had as much respect for the two men as Brink did, which wasn't much. "We don't pick who we protect," he said. Brink understood exactly what he meant.

Minutes later Brink found himself in the Oval Office with Abraham and President Richard Wilson. After shaking hands and the usual small talk, they sat down and the President began.

"Vice President Thornburg wanted to be here but got called away on an urgent matter. He sends his deepest regards to you, Mr. Brink. He wanted me to convey to you how highly he thinks of you for what you have done for our nation."

Brink genuinely welcomed the gratitude. "Well, thank you sir, those kind words mean a lot. It's always nice to be appreciated."

"I share his opinion. You have given more to this nation than any of us could ask of you. I'm sure you know my predecessor and I did not see eye to eye on many things, but I think you can agree that I have continued his policy of giving you the support you need. Am I right?"

Brink knew President Richard Wilson to be one of the greatest liars in American political history, but on this point he was telling the stone cold truth. "Yes sir, I can honestly say you both have shown us support and have kept our activities discreet. For that, I am grateful."

"Good, I am glad to hear you say that. Good."

Brink knew a setup when he saw one. Wilson was buttering him up, but for what?

While the President stood a young looking 50, Director Donald Abraham was an old looking 70. Inside his body felt great, but on the outside he looked like he could barely walk. The word around town spread that his initials "D.A," stood for "don't ask." He knew where the bodies were buried going back a long time. No President dared to be dumb enough or courageous enough to try and fire him. He just kept chugging along. When he left government, it would be on his own terms.

Abraham's cold stare unnerved most people, but Brink took it in stride. "Aldo, the President and I are very worried about you. I asked him to have this meeting because I have concerns."

Brink knew exactly what would come next. "About me retiring?" he asked.

The President let out a chuckle. "Are you ever surprised by anything, Mr. Brink?"

"Sir, if I am surprised, it means I'm dead. So no, not usually."

"Good point. The director came to me and told me that he is concerned that you will retire soon, leaving us with a gaping hole in our ability to deal with our most severe threats. This meeting is to convince you to stay at least a while longer. It will take at least five full trained agents to replace you in the program, and as you know, we don't have them. This deeply concerns me, the Vice President, and Director Abraham."

This pissed Brink off, but he didn't let on. He had told Abraham in a private conversation a few months ago that he started to think about retiring sometime soon, but gave no indication of what soon meant. Apparently, it must have freaked out the old man to the point where he called the President.

Brink chose his words carefully. "Sir, I assure you that I have decided no such thing as of yet, and it's premature for you or the Director to worry about it. When I do make the decision I will give plenty of notice and help in whatever way I can to smooth the transition."

"Glad to hear it," Wilson said.

"But, you should know something. I will not do this forever. If I want to move on, that's what will happen. I've paid my dues."

"And then some," Abraham said. The President nodded.

"Well, then I won't keep you Mr. Brink. I apologize for asking you to come in on your day off, but we needed to address this."

"No problem, I had to go out to run some errands anyway." The men stood up and shook hands.

"Mr. Brink, there is one more thing."

"Yes?"

"I would like to invite you to our party this Saturday."

"That's very nice, but after taking today and tomorrow off, I will be buried in work."

"I won't take no for an answer and have already told the director here that you are to be excused for a third day to attend this event. I want you to know how much you are appreciated by this administration even if we can't say so publicly."

"Only if I can bring my girlfriend," Brink said.

"Of course, bring her along." The President always perked up whenever the topic of women came up. He and the Vice President had more mistresses than Brink had false identities, which made it an impressive and disgusting number all at once.

What the President didn't know was that by Saturday Jazlyn would no longer just be his girlfriend. She would be his fiancée, and their first date after being engaged would be a Presidential party.

As Brink walked out, the President grabbed his arm and pulled him in close. "Is it serious?" the President asked.

"As DEFCON 1."

"Take it from me, women are nothing but trouble," Wilson said.

Brink could barely hold in his laughter. Jazlyn was nothing like the slimy hookers and sycophants the President had relations with. Abraham started shaking his head behind Wilson's back indicating to Brink he should just let it go.

"We'll see you Saturday, sir."

CHAPTER 3

Aldo Brink showered for the second time that day and put on his perfectly clean two button black suit. Barring something catastrophic, he would be engaged in a few hours. He reached into his pocket and double checked that the ring was safe and secure inside its box. He took a deep breath and headed out.

Rush hour had just ended, so traffic was light as he swiftly changed lanes in his BMW. He stopped off to buy Jazlyn some flowers from the conveniently located florist a few blocks from her condo. When he pulled up to her place, he wasn't nervous. He felt exhilarated.

He walked up the few steps and rang the doorbell. When the door opened a moment later Jazlyn Reyes emerged wearing a red dress that accentuated her best parts. The slit up the side and the legs that had caught Brink's eye two years ago had returned, as had her exotic

Jimmy Choo heels. Like two years ago, they matched the dress perfectly.

"You look stunning as always," Brink said. He handed her the dozen red roses he had just picked up.

"They are beautiful Aldo, and they go perfectly with my dress! How did you know what I was wearing?"

Brink had no idea what she would be wearing, but played it cool. "I have spies everywhere. Shall we go? We are going somewhere special tonight." Jazlyn went inside for a brief second to drop off the flowers, but she kept one rose with her and smelled it seductively as Brink drove them to the National Arboretum.

"If I knew we were going here, I would have worn something different! You know this is one of my favorite places, but I need good walking shoes, hon. Why did you tell me to wear something special if we are just going to walk around this place?"

"Patience, Jaz," Brink said.

The arboretum fell just outside downtown Washington and had an impressive assortment of beautiful gardens. They parked and began walking to the entrance. The parking lot was completely empty and when they reached the entrance they found the gates locked. The sign with the hours said it had closed over two hours ago.

"I guess we should have gotten here earlier," Jazlyn said with a smile and a wink.

Brink checked his watch. "Nah, we're good." The second he said it a middle aged uniformed security guard shuffled up to the gate, and unlocked it.

"Mr. Brink, welcome to the National Arboretum. I am proud to present this special viewing to you and your guest. Please proceed to the Capitol Columns and enjoy your evening," said the gentlemanly guard.

Brink held his arm out and a clearly intrigued Jazlyn took it. They walked arm in arm to the Capitol Columns area of the Arboretum. It was probably the most beautiful part of the living museum. As they got closer, Jazlyn saw a large reflecting pool with stone steps leading up to several majestic columns just like the ones found at countless government buildings and monuments in Washington. Flowers were sparsely situated among the columns and in the water. She had been here before, but something seemed different this time. Small lit candles lined the stone steps and along the top edge of the reflecting pool.

A few days earlier Brink journeyed to the arboretum to find the late night security guard. He explained what he wanted to do and paid the guard and the late night groundskeeper five hundred dollars each to help him out. Their jobs weren't exactly filled with excitement, so they were happy to do something fun for a change. The five hundred didn't hurt, either.

After overcoming a bit of shock, Jazlyn realized what was going on, but could only muster a series of sighs and deep breaths. Her emotions overwhelmed her as she realized that Aldo had gone to so much trouble. Brink led her to the top of the steps. The clear night and comfortable temperature made the evening complete. The moon reflected in the crystal clear water of the reflecting pool.

Everything looked perfect, and just how Brink planned. The only variable he couldn't control was the weather and he checked the three day forecast earlier in the week before he made these plans. *Thank you Mr. Weatherman.*

Brink took her hand and looked directly into her eyes, exactly like the first time they met.

"I have dedicated my life to something bigger than myself, as you know, but I know now that you are the most important thing in my life and that will never change. I love you with all my heart and soul. You mean more to me than I could ever put into words, but I will try by asking you this…"

Jazlyn put her hand over her mouth in a futile gesture designed to contain her euphoria. Aldo Brink took a knee and pulled a small box from his pocket. He opened it revealing a brilliant diamond ring.

"Jazlyn Reyes, will you marry me?"

"Oh my God Yes! I love you!"

Before Brink could even stand up, Jazlyn had her arms wrapped around him. She kissed him and squeezed him with all her might. As they continued their embrace a man slowly approached them with a bottle of champagne and two glasses. The late night groundskeeper had a smile on his face almost as big as Jazlyn's.

"Ah, Mr. Brink, I trust you received the answer you were looking for." The man poured them some champagne and left the chilled bottle on the steps in an ice bucket. "I bid you goodnight, and congratulations." With that, the diminutive groundskeeper retrieved two small pillows from behind a nearby tree, placed them on the top step, and disappeared into the night.

Aldo Brink had spent years dealing with the scum of the Earth. His crusade took its toll. His body was scarred and his mind had begun to suffer as well after so many years of torture. Just when he thought he had enough, this perfect angel appeared to him in a black dress at a party he didn't even want to be at. It must have been fate, he thought. Luck could not possibly explain how fortunate he felt at this moment sitting on the steps near the reflecting pool with Jazlyn.

He had seen men treat their wives and mistresses alike as disposable pleasures. He saw firsthand, including at 1600 Pennsylvania Avenue, how marriages were often ones of convenience entered into for status or political expediency. Brink knew this would be different. This was real. Every time he saw her, a jolt coursed through his body. It had been like that ever since he met her. They clicked on every level. He would never want anyone else. Brink leaned over and kissed her again as they raised their champagne flutes and toasted their future together.

The newly engaged couple kissed again, sipped their champagne, and stared across the water in an unforgettable embrace.

CHAPTER 4

The next day and a half flew by like a blur. Brink had no family and no close friends who were still alive, so the next day was spent making calls to Jazlyn's family and friends. Her family lived in Miami and rejoiced at the news.

They had spent some time with Brink over the last two years when they came up to visit her. He even accompanied her down to Miami to attend the funeral of her grandmother who lived to 101. Needless to say, this earned him plenty of praise from her very conservative religious family. They saw him helping the family around the house and with errands during the wake and funeral. Brink always made sure everyone else was taken care of, and always paid extra attention to Jazlyn during their time of grief. Her family noticed.

While her mother Marisol spoke English fluently along with her native Portuguese, Jazlyn's father Juan spoke just enough to communicate, but preferred his native language or the Spanish which he picked up in Miami. Working as a deep cover operative for many years across the globe meant Brink needed to study multiple languages and cultures. He spoke Italian, German, Arabic, Farsi, and Spanish. Being able to converse with Juan Reyes in Spanish was a big help in convincing him that he would always treat his daughter with respect and always take care of her. Upon hearing the news of their engagement, Juan insisted on throwing them a lavish engagement party in Miami.

Juan Reyes ran a successful Brazilian restaurant in Miami for thirty-two years that provided a good life for his family after arriving in America with his wife and young daughter. He sold the restaurant and retired just last year. Both of Jazlyn's parents were wonderful people, not to mention fantastic cooks. Brink looked forward to seeing them, and their food.

Brink didn't want to go to this Presidential party. It was a silly affair where big shots patted each other on the back and talked about how great they were. He would rather stay home with his new fiancée. Presidential demand or not, Brink was more than willing to blow it off, but Jazlyn convinced him to go. She wanted to tell everyone at the party about their engagement and how happy she felt. Brink's resistance to the idea crumbled as he saw the giant smile on his fiancée's face.

Before he knew it, they were dancing in the middle of a ballroom very similar to the one where they met. Brink didn't even know what purpose this party served. From the looks of it he deduced it was a thank you to the President's most generous donors which gave these people the opportunity to drink champagne with people in government so they could curry special favor. *As if they needed it.*

None of that mattered though. Brink saw how happy Jazlyn looked. She glowed with a radiance that beamed brilliantly, even for her, as she worked the room. She knew many of the people there from her work with the ESCP and looked more than happy to share her glorious news with every single one of them. This night, she wore a glorious white dress that foreshadowed their wedding day, he thought.

"Oh my, he is so handsome, Jaz!" Brink could read the ladies' lips from across the room.

"Oh yes he is!" she said.

The ring sparkled, as Jazlyn held her hand up to her friends.

"Does he have a brother?" one of her friends asked.

"Nope, and he's all mine," she said.

Brink saw Vice President Jerry Thornburg walking towards him. Thornburg possessed a loud personality, and never seemed to modulate his voice even if the setting required it. That was probably why the White House advisors hardly ever let him give public speeches.

Given the work he had done over the years, Brink found himself the recipient of quite a bit of sensitive information. He knew the dirty secrets both personal and professional of the power brokers in town. Those same people tried desperately to keep the truth under wraps.

While Brink knew President Wilson to be a skilled liar and adulterer, he still believed that in his heart of hearts Richard Wilson strived to do right by the American people. He cared about his country, and its history.

Thornburg however, was a different story. The man seemed to be along for the ride. The son of a media tycoon and heir to more than four billion dollars, Jerry Thornburg was handed everything on a silver platter from birth. He liked to drink, and party, in that order. Partying usually meant acting like a fool, surrounding himself with female groupies, and partaking in some recreational drug use.

Brink knew there had been top government officials with some moral failings, but this was off the charts. The Vice President of the Unite States was literally a drunkard who occasionally used cocaine. Obviously, the White House kept this secret, but while the spin was that Thornburg operated as a dedicated public servant who assisted the President on every issue, the truth was that Thornburg did almost nothing. The President knew he was a flake who could bring down the whole administration. Had they asked him to resign, Thornburg would have gone scorched Earth and taken the whole place down with him.

Instead, the White House let him have his fun as long as he stayed out of their serious policy affairs. It was an arrangement that apparently had worked. The only reason Jerry Thornburg was on the ticket was that it gave the campaign access to his personal family fortune and would guarantee positive media coverage from the Thornburg family media empire. He was like a drunken college frat boy on Spring Break, except he wore an expensive suit, and Spring Break lasted his whole life.

"Aldo, I mean Mr. Brink, so glad you could make it!" Thornburg said, with a glassy look in his eyes.

Brink extended his hand. Thornburg switched his cocktail from his right hand to his left and then extended his. "Thank you for the invitation, Mr. Vice President. Jazlyn is really enjoying herself."

"Is that her over there?"

Brink nodded.

"Then you are a very lucky man. I heard her and some of the ladies talking. Is it true you are engaged?"

"Yes, I asked her Thursday night at the Arboretum."

Thornburg seemed impressed. "So you did it classy, huh? Well, good for you. I'm happy for you both. You deserve the happiness that my wife and I have."

Brink couldn't believe what he just heard. The marriage between Jerry and Lucy Thornburg was a political sham designed to make him appear respectable. Lucy saw other men on the side and she knew Jerry had multiple mistresses. Once the administration had served two terms, Lucy would divorce him and walk away with a large settlement. In the meantime, it was all business.

Brink just nodded and smiled.

"I must congratulate your lovely fiancée as well. Enjoy yourself tonight." With that Jerry Thornburg walked across the room and gave Jazlyn a hug. Brink could not hear what was said but it looked above board, and Thornburg soon moved on. Jazlyn and the few other women she spoke to turned, smiled, and waved back at Brink.

Everything was working out. Brink would work a few more years, save some money, then retire and live out his days with his dream woman. If he got bored he could always become an instructor of some kind, but he couldn't fathom how traveling and enjoying life with Jazlyn Reyes would ever become boring. Maybe they would start a family? They had talked about it and decided that it would be best to wait until Brink retired.

After an hour of mingling, Brink lost track of Jazlyn. He walked around the massive ballroom but there was no sign of her. He asked a few people who she had been talking with and they said a Secret Service agent asked her to step away for a moment, because the Vice President needed her advice. Brink's mind cranked up at the sound of this. Jerry Thornburg could not to be trusted around any woman, especially not when they were alone.

Before worrying too much he quickly came to the conclusion that all the Vice President wanted was some advice on selling the new Energy Bill to Congress which had been stalled for weeks. Brink had read about it in the paper that very morning. It had been the hot issue being debated in the Beltway.

Just the same though, he wanted to find her. The music stopped playing. The band announced they were taking a break and the dance floor soon cleared. Brink looked around and moved to the right side of the hall.

A terrifying scream pierced the air. Loud gasps and cries erupted from the crowd. Brink instinctively ran towards the back of the hall, from where he thought he heard it. Secret Service agents had formed a perimeter and were attempting to hold back the crowd. Two wide doors were open that led to what looked like some kind of executive office. Face up on the desk lay the body of Vice President Jerry Thornburg, his white shirt half unbuttoned and stained with blood. What looked to be a letter opener had been thrust into his neck. Brink knew he was dead.

As paramedics rushed in trying hopelessly to revive him, Brink's eyes scanned left and saw his fiancée Jazlyn Reyes on her knees, with her wrists handcuffed behind her back. The front of her white dress had blood on it. Her hair looked awful and she looked like she'd been in a struggle. Her face said it all. She was terrified.

CHAPTER 5

Jazlyn had been whisked away by the Secret Service and he hadn't been able to speak to her. Brink thought their eyes might have met for a moment as they ushered her out, but the look on her face indicated that shock had set in. At that moment, she wasn't able to see him or anything else.

Brink raced to his car. He wasn't entirely sure what to do. He knew he had to make some calls to find out where she was taken, and get a lawyer for her immediately. Brink prayed that she would ask for a lawyer right away, but given the circumstances he wasn't real optimistic about the FBI or Secret Service adhering to protocol and ending the interrogation when she invoked her right to counsel.

Brink already figured he knew what happened. That prick Thornburg was high as a kite, tried to force himself on her, and she grabbed the letter opener off the desk and stabbed him. It was clear cut self-defense. What other explanation could there be, Brink wondered? The Vice

President was notorious for this kind of shit, but it was always covered up for political reasons. This time he picked the wrong woman. Jazlyn was not a groupie enamored with the power and prestige of the office.

Brink knew how this would play out. If the investigation was fair, there would be no question his fiancée would be coming home, but he knew that was a fantasy. There would be nothing fair about this. If it came out that Thornburg tried to rape her and she killed him in self-defense, it would bring the whole administration down. The media would dig into Thornburg like never before and all his mistresses would come out of the woodwork. The President couldn't say he knew nothing about his unstable Vice President, and he would be toast.

All this was speculation on Brink's part. He still hadn't spoken to her and asked, "What happened?" But right then and there, he was ready to bet his life on one thing. His fiancée was not a killer.

"Damn!" Brink shouted to himself as he continually reached people's voice mails while on the way to his car. Realizing he had to get out of there before traffic totally backed up, or before the roads were closed, he slammed the car into reverse, spun the wheel, narrowly missed hitting another car, and sped off into the night running a red light in the process.

He wasn't reaching anyone, because most were asleep or were being awakened this very minute. His bosses and the entire security apparatus of the United States would be in panic mode trying to figure out if this was a coordinated terrorist attack and if the threat was ongoing. *I have to find her.*

"Call Taylor Ross," Brink said calmly. He could hear the phone ringing on his BMW's speakers since his phone was connected via Bluetooth.

"Aldo, what's up? I just heard the VP is dead. What's the deal, bro?"

Taylor Ross hardly ever slept. He was the no name unit's technology specialist, and a certified genius. He was 29, but looked like a 16 year old surfer from Malibu. He had graduated early from MIT with a perfect GPA, and had Master's Degrees in Software Engineering and Mechanical Engineering. He practically lived at Langley and barely went home at all. He could have made ten times per year what he made at the CIA, but he genuinely loved his work, and he loved being able to work on new tech stuff with what amounted to an unlimited budget.

"Taylor, listen carefully. I need to know exactly where they are interrogating the woman they arrested for killing Thornburg."

"Got it, if it's in a system or in the airwaves, it's mine. Call you back in five?"

"Thanks, Taylor. Please hurry." The phone went dead. Brink pulled the car over and took a deep breath. He was confident Taylor would find out where she was. He never even asked Brink why he wanted to know this information. All he knew was that Aldo Brink said it was urgent, and if he said that, it meant something major was going down. They were not supposed to be involved in this sort of thing, so Taylor knew to deny they even had a conversation if asked.

Brink waited in silence for what seemed like an eternity, but after a few minutes the phone rang. He answered it immediately.

"Found it. It wasn't anywhere in a database yet, but I picked up the radio traffic. Prisoner Jazlyn Reyes is being interviewed at Third District Station, 1624 V Street Northwest."

"I know where that is, but why a local police station?"

"Radio traffic said when the Attorney General was informed he went ballistic and said she had to be taken to a nearby local detention facility where the local authorities would hold her until the FBI arrived," Ross explained.

"I want to get there before the FBI does, how much time do I have?" Brink spun the tires of his BMW as he sped off. He could be there in five to ten minutes if he hurried.

"I'm tracking them now, bro. FBI is ten to twelve minutes out. You can beat them. Just haul ass."

"I'm on my way. Thanks for the help," Brink said.

"Anytime bro, you need anything, hit me up."

"Listen Taylor, you're going to hear a lot of shit about what went down tonight. Don't believe it. It's all bullshit. Jazlyn Reyes didn't kill him, and if she did it was self-defense. OK?"

"Yeah man, you don't have to worry about me. I trust you over the media and the politicians every damn day, no doubt…Just curious, but, how do you know?"

"She's my fiancée."

"Oh, shit."

"Yeah, I know. Listen, I'm almost there. Keep your eyes and ears open, OK?"

"You got it. Be safe, bro."

Brink double parked outside the police station and grabbed a briefcase from the trunk of his BMW before walking quickly into the station past a few Secret Service agents. Brink went into character immediately. He had been undercover with the most ruthless crime syndicates, terrorist organizations, and drug empires that existed on Earth, so this should be easy. The problem was this time his emotions were involved. He did his best to block them out as he reached the front desk.

"Excuse me! You all must have taken the academy course on Gestapo tactics, because there is no other explanation as to why my client is being interrogated without her lawyer present!" Brink yelled with just the right amount of smarm.

A man Brink identified as the Captain walked over. "Sir, your client is in the interrogation room. The FBI will be here momentarily and will question her. She has not said a word since she arrived and has not invoked her right to counsel," the Captain said sounding like he had recited that line a thousand times.

"If you don't let me see my client this instant, I will guarantee that you will go down in history as the policeman who invalidated the entire case against her by violating her constitutional rights!"

Brink wasn't trying to make an actual legal argument. All he wanted to do was talk to her for a few minutes before the situation got out of hand. The Captain seemed to want to get this over with and knowing the FBI would be there any minute, he escorted Brink to the interrogation room. "Your lawyer is here." The Captain left and closed the door behind him.

Jazlyn had a bruise on her cheek and was still wearing her blood stained clothes. When Jazlyn looked and saw the man she loved, she jumped from her chair and hugged him. It didn't feel like she would ever let go. Brink tried to comfort her.

"I'm here, Jaz. I'm going to take care of everything. I love you. You just need to be strong now."

"Aldo, he tried to rape me. I felt so weak. I was almost blacking out. He must have put something in my drink. I tried to scream, but no one could hear me over the music. His hands were around my throat. I was so scared," Jazlyn said, with tears in her eyes.

Brink noticed the bruise on her neck and cheek. He took his smartphone out and snapped a few pictures of them and made sure the photos made it clear she was at the police station. They would be helpful during a trial, he thought. "It was self-defense, I know. I knew right away," Brink said.

Jazlyn finally let go of him and paced around. "I was just swinging my arms around trying to grab anything to hit him with. I must have grabbed the letter opener and stabbed him. It's all a haze to me."

"I know Jaz. You're in shock and if he drugged you, you can't think clearly."

"What am I going to do? My life is over. Our life together is over!" Jazlyn said. She started to shake. The shock was wearing off and the full gravity of what happened had started to sink in. Brink grabbed her by the shoulders.

"No! Your life is not over and neither is ours. We are going to make it through this, I promise you. I'm going to find you a great lawyer and do everything I can. The FBI will be here any minute to question you. The second they do, tell them you want to speak to a lawyer. If they persist, say nothing. Wait until the lawyer I hire finds you. Then tell him everything you told me. OK?"

"OK, I got it."

"I love you Jaz, and I promise you, they aren't going to take you away from me."

Brink had to go. He didn't want to be there when the FBI arrived. Now was not the time to confront them directly. Brink kissed her gently and said he would see her soon. He told her again to be strong, and to say nothing until she met with her lawyer.

Brink stormed out of the police station while shouting at the Captain.

"My client has invoked her right to remain silent. She will not speak to you or anyone else until my colleague meets with her. You better let her get cleaned up or I will have all your fucking badges!"

Outside, Aldo Brink sped away. In his rearview mirror, he saw the flashing lights of the unmarked FBI vehicles as they arrived at the station.

CHAPTER 6

Gloria Smith stepped out of her dazzling blue chiffon dress revealing black stockings and garters with a matching set of bra and panties as she gazed out the window of her hotel room. Her fair skin and slender athletic body reflected in the glass as her piercing blue eyes watched the chaos below. She slipped off her black Christian Louboutin heels first, then her stockings, before admiring the rose tattoo just above her left ankle.

Across the street, hundreds of people were congregating outside the convention center where Vice President Jerry Thornburg's dead body had just been removed and driven away. Flashing lights filled the night as cars jockeyed for position trying to get through the crush of people who had spilled out into the street.

She felt a special thrill as she watched the people scurry about beneath her. It was quite a sight to behold. History was unfolding in front of her. Their screams of terror were her handiwork. Now, she bathed in their grief and loved every second of it.

A knock at the door made her turn her head. She walked slowly to the door and opened it. The tall man who entered wore a dark suit and earpiece with a wire running down inside his jacket. She turned her back to him and walked away slowly toward the bottle of vodka that stood next to the ice bucket where two glasses sat. She dropped two cubes of ice into each glass, and poured some vodka into each one. The man kept his eyes on her thong and her perfectly formed ass as he quietly closed the door, locking it behind him.

"Looks like we had a little surprise tonight," the tall man said as he came up behind her and grabbed her waist.

"An opportunity presented itself." She purred as the man worked his hands up her body.

"Well, we'll just see where this takes us then, won't we?"

CHAPTER 7

The next day, Brink met with Sam Hodges at CIA Headquarters in Langley. Hodges' office was more lavish than even the Director's and Brink had always wondered why. A short, thin man who always appeared white as a ghost, Hodges had started losing his hair. Having just turned 45, he required reading glasses.

"What do you know?" Hodges asked.

"I know this is bullshit. What do you know?"

"Come on, Aldo. What do you know?"

It had been less than a minute, and Hodges had already exhausted Brink's patience. He liked and respected the Deputy Director, but he also knew him to be an ambitious political type who had taken great care in positioning himself for the director's chair when Donald Abraham's inevitable retirement came to pass. The last thing Hodges wanted was to go up against the administration, especially on such a high profile event.

"She went into a room with him, he tried to rape her while high as a kite, and she stabbed the bastard in the neck in self-defense."

"How do you know this?"

"She told me," Brink said.

"When?"

"Last night at the Third District Station before the FBI showed up."

Hodges furrowed his brow and rubbed his head. "So you were the lawyer I heard about? He stormed in and started ranting and raving about the Constitution before her actual attorney showed up later that night."

"I have no idea what you're talking about."

"OK." Hodges didn't believe him, but felt it was best to let it drop.

"I see where this is headed, Sam," Brink said. "And I can promise you right now Jazlyn Reyes is not going to rot away in prison for the rest of her life for defending herself from a drug addict rapist."

"That's not up to you, Aldo."

We'll see.

"Right now the evidence is overwhelming from what I've seen. Forget that she is your fiancée for a minute and just examine the evidence. She is found at the scene with her fingerprints on the murder weapon, and she has drugs in her system."

"What drugs? It's too soon for you to have that kind of information from a toxicology report."

"It hasn't been released yet, but it's true."

That seemed awful fast to Brink. Something didn't smell right. "She must have been drugged."

"It doesn't appear so," Hodges said.

"How about this evidence?" Brink held his smart phone up. The pictures of the bruises on Jazlyn's neck and cheek made no impression from the blank stare on the Deputy Director's face. "Let me guess, the police, FBI, or Secret Service never took photos of her face and when they heal, no one will remember them. Am I getting warm?"

"Those would certainly help her case when it comes to self-defense, but…"

"But what?"

"You know it's not enough." Hodges was right. They had no evidence to prove her innocence and unless something turned up, it would be impossible to get her off. The investigation would be a sick joke designed to protect the Vice President's sham image, and by extension, the administration. If any evidence was to be unearthed, it would be Brink who would have to do it.

The feeling of dread in the pit of his stomach told him one thing. He would fail.

CHAPTER 8

Earlier that morning, Gloria Smith heard the shower running as she lay in bed. She had waited a long time for this kind of opportunity and performed her duty when the moment came. Her country could be proud of her for the service she provided, she thought. Of course, she knew her actions and that of her lover could never be revealed publicly, but that didn't mean she couldn't reap the rewards from completing her top secret assignment, and ahead of schedule no less.

As her lover showered, she couldn't help but think about him. He had fair skin like her, was tall, handsome, and had the rugged good looks of a fit Marine. They had worked together in close proximity for the last ten months and he had fallen in love with her. She was drawn to him physically, but Gloria Smith was not a woman who fell in love. She never understood the emotion. To her, there was no difference between love, and physical gratification. After she was done with him, he would be disposed of, just like the countless men that came before him.

She loved to feel the adrenalin course through her veins as a mission reached its climax. As a couple, they were addicted to danger. They fed off of it. Their whole relationship was based on it. Gloria Smith barely felt anything anymore and found that in order to be stimulated she had to keep pushing the envelope.

Lucky for her, she was given the opportunity to do just that. Her profession was a daily dose of life threatening situations where she would get to decide who lives and who dies. She was a queen of ice, both in appearance with her fair skin, and more importantly, with her total disregard for everyone but herself.

As her tall lover emerged from the bathroom wearing only a towel, she let out a sensual sigh loud enough for him to hear it. It was only for his benefit.

"You're not the only one who likes what they see," he said.

She was about to reply with something witty, when her cell phone on the night stand next to her started buzzing. The caller ID indicated it was her employer.

The other voice on the phone was deep and raspy to the point where if you didn't know it you would think the man was using a voice changer. Gloria had met the man and knew better. It was just how he spoke on the phone when business was being conducted.

"He was expected to pass on next week. The client is not happy."

"An opportunity presented itself for liquidation. I took it."

"Yes, I suppose in today's market you have to act when you see an opportunity, but the client is very upset. He said he might demand a meeting sometime soon depending on the fallout."

"Why is he upset?" Gloria asked.

"We were supposed to clear the name with him. I hope to learn more today. Keep a low profile until you are contacted again." The line went dead.

"What was that about?" her lover asked.

"He said the client is upset. I presume with the timing."

Her lover quickly slipped on a pair of jeans and a flannel shirt before cozying up next to her in bed. "Well, he'll just have to learn to live with disappointment."

CHAPTER 9

As the months passed, Brink's fears had been confirmed. This wasn't an investigation; it was a show trial in the making. He had found one of the best high profile criminal attorneys on the East Coast who agreed to take the case pro bono. He was a camera whore, Brink thought, but at the top of his profession none the less. He won more than he lost, but given the situation, Brink knew deep down that even the best legal magician wasn't going to pull a rabbit out of this hat. The case transfixed the whole nation, and the people wanted blood. They needed someone to be punished. The "news" media made it even worse, he thought.

If that wasn't bad enough, Brink had learned some things that put the whole investigation into question. The only pieces of evidence that appeared uncorrupted were the pictures that he snapped of Jazlyn's bruises. Her lawyer said they would be helpful in crafting her defense and commended Brink for his quick thinking. There were other problems, however.

The investigation, if it could be called that, had produced a toxicology report saying both Jazlyn and Thornburg had cocaine in their system. Brink came by the information from Taylor Ross, whom he had asked to grab everything out there from the investigation and send it to him digitally. With Taylor's help, Brink knew almost everything about the case and passed as much as he could to Jazlyn's lawyer.

The Vice President doing coke made sense. He looked high at the party. Practically anyone could see that if they knew what to look for; but Jazlyn? Brink had known her for two years and she barely took so much as an aspirin. Furthering his suspicions were numerous leaks from the Secret Service and FBI to the media. These leaks painted Jazlyn as a junkie and the only one with drugs in her system.

The lie had begun to take shape. The administration needed Jerry Thornburg to be the victim and the recipient of the nation's grief. If the true story of the drugs and attempted rape came out, the whole administration would come crashing down. People would rightly ask the President what he knew and when he knew it. Did he know about the Vice President's drug use and womanizing, and if so why did he cover it up and allow it to continue? The flip side was just as bad. He could say he didn't know anything about it which would make him seem incompetent and unable to see what was going on right in front of his face with the man he chose to be his running mate. The administration would go down in flames. To save it, they had to make Jazlyn the villain of the story.

All they had for her defense were the pictures Brink had taken. The evidence of cocaine in her system was certainly falsified Brink thought, but how could they prove it in court? At the end of the day, it would be Jazlyn's word on the witness stand that he attempted to rape her. The media and politicians would go ballistic and call her a slut who was dishonoring a public servant who couldn't defend himself. The Secret Service agents would testify that they heard a scream and when they opened the doors, the Vice President was dead. There were no security cameras inside the office, but there were many inside the ballroom that connected to it.

The security footage clearly showed Jazlyn being led to the office by a Secret Service agent whose face Brink couldn't see. The footage also showed Thornburg and her each getting a drink from the bar, and then going back into the office with the doors closing behind them. Taylor Ross was analyzing all the footage to try and see if anything had been altered. So far, he hadn't found anything to indicate tampering. He promised Brink he would keep working and turn over every digital rock in the case to try and find something to help his fiancée. Brink appreciated the young kid sticking his neck out for him like that.

Brink knew he was running out of options. The trial would be starting soon, but the outcome was predetermined. Brink thought about going public with what he found out about the drugs and Jazlyn's lawyer considered it as well, but in the end it would just come off as insane ramblings by people desperate to save her. The fact was they had no proof.

He had barely slept in months. He was tormented by the image of his angel Jazlyn being confined to a cell. Despite her lawyer's best effort, she had been ordered held without bail for the duration of the trial. Brink was ready to take out two mortgages on his house to bail her out, but he never got the chance.

When he did sleep, he awoke in cold sweats after vicious nightmares of Jazlyn suffering in prison. She was being held in the new state of the art Wilson Federal Prison Complex in Virginia, outside Washington. It had been built only a few years ago and had already received two reports on 60 Minutes about abuse being committed against the inmates, especially the female ones.

Jazlyn was segregated in the maximum security wing of the female section. Approximately 15% of the population was female, in a facility that held over 200 inmates. Normally, a female prisoner would not be held in such a high level facility, but due to the high profile nature of the case she was segregated and locked down 23 hours a day. She was allowed one hour outside per day in a fenced off area where she would be the only person with the exception of the guards outside the fence and in the towers.

Because this facility was not meant for people currently going through trial, visiting her was especially difficult. No physical contact was allowed. Their visits took place through an inch of soundproof ballistic glass. They spoke through a telephone receiver. Each time Brink saw the love of his life in that awful orange jumpsuit he seethed with rage. He was a master of his emotions and did an admirable job of staying strong in front of her. He told her it would all be OK and they would be together somehow.

"My life is over, Aldo! Don't you see that!?" Jazlyn screamed.

"Quiet down, or I will remove you," said the guard who looked to be enjoying himself.

"I talked to your parents again. They want to come and see you."

"No, I don't want them seeing me like this. I don't even want you seeing me like this."

"Jaz, we love you. We…..."

"Time's up." The guard was back again barking orders. After declaring their time was up, he grabbed Jazlyn a bit too forcefully for Brink's taste and pulled her away.

Aldo Brink committed the man's face to memory. In that instant, had he been on the other side of the glass, the guard would have been a dead man.

CHAPTER 10

Taylor Ross always worked late. His office at Langley was more like a studio apartment in a secluded area of the complex. He had his own private bathroom, kitchen, and sleeping area. It wasn't luxurious, but he liked to be left alone so it worked for him. Aldo Brink was the only person in or out of the no name unit that he got along with, though he did work with others when he had to.

His very own satellite completed the amenities of his office. It belonged to the no name unit, but he was its keeper. He had repositioned it from its assigned mission over the Middle East to monitor a variety of things inside DC and the surrounding area. He wasn't sure what he was looking for, but he would know it when he found it.

He often laughed with Brink about this being his bachelor pad. While Taylor might have looked like the tech geek without a date, he actually did quite well in that department. He had a studio outside work that he rented so people could see he had a real place to live. Meeting women at bars was never a problem and he had the reputation as quite the smooth talker. Brink warned him many times that while tempting, he should never tell anyone who he worked for and what he did in order to impress them. He told him just to say you were a technology consultant and leave it at that. Taylor followed Brink's advice to the letter.

He worked countless hours trying to piece everything together. He examined everything the government said would put Jazlyn away. That was the only way to ultimately deconstruct it completely. He had to understand how it came together. His fingers flew across two different keyboards as he analyzed every report and radio transmission from the investigation.

The massive amounts of data reflected in his eyeglasses as he waited for Brink's call. The call would come in any minute and Taylor was thrilled that he finally had something to tell him. When the phone rang, he told him the news.

"Taylor, please tell me you have something."

"The toxicology report that I thought was the original is a digital copy."

"Where's the original?"

"Hell if I know, but I can tell you the report they have been showing all over the TV is a digital copy that's been altered. When I examined it, I found a discrepancy."

"What kind of discrepancy?"

"In the report you can tell every section is original except for the areas that discuss the drugs in their systems.

Those sections have a new digital layer imprinted over them. I tried to see what was there originally, but it's impossible."

"This sounds like a lot of techno bullshit. Could you testify in court that the report has been altered?" Brink asked.

"In simple terms, part of the report is a fake."

"Can you testify to that in court?"

"Absolutely, but Hodges told me I would not be permitted to testify. He said the company and the White House would invoke something about state secrets preventing me from doing it and if I show up I will be arrested. He must have known you would ask me for help, but he can't prove that's what we are doing. I've covered all my tracks. These assholes couldn't find a hooker in a whorehouse without me."

"That piece of shit."

"Don't sweat it bro, I'm there. Just tell me when to show up. Even if they arrest me, it will make all the papers and my testimony will get out there. It won't be admissible in court, but it still could help, right?

Brink, though touched by the gesture, dismissed it. "No reason your life should be ruined, too. Is there anything else?"

Taylor Ross was about to speak when he heard something rumble outside the door of his office. He put his Bluetooth earpiece in and walked to the door. A loud bang stopped him in his tracks. Retreating to his desk, he opened a drawer and punched in the code to the small safe inside.

He pulled his Walther P99QA Compact 9mm pistol from the safe and racked the slide. Walking back to the door with a round in the chamber, he was relaxed as could be.

"Hang on bro, something's up here." Taylor came to the door and listened. Hearing nothing, he flung the door open revealing a tall night janitor who was repacking his cart after it had apparently fallen over.

"I am so sorry for disturbing you, sir. I was hoping no one was working late when I tipped my cart over," the janitor said, pleading for forgiveness.

"Don't sweat it. Just try to keep it down."

The shamed janitor never raised his head, and continued picking up his supplies as Taylor closed his door and returned to the office. He continued with Brink.

"Sorry about that. I thought it was on."

"You sure, it's fine?" Brink asked.

"Yeah. Listen, there is another reason why I think it's a fake."

"What is it?"

"The original pathologist is dead. He was killed in an attempted mugging a block from his house. The new pathologist was just handed all of the old guy's stuff. It would have been real easy to replace the old one and the new guy would have no reason to question it. The work was done. It's pretty convenient for the guy to die in a mugging right after he made the so called original report, huh?"

"Keep on it. Thanks again man," Brink said.

"You got it, bro. I'm still working on all the angles of the surveillance footage. Watch your six out there." Taylor hung up the phone and started to put his Walther back in his desk safe, but at the last second decided against it. Instead, he simply laid it on the desk. He looked back at his office door one last time. "I gotta put a camera out there," he said to himself.

In the hallway, Gloria Smith's tall lover pushed his janitorial cart down the hallway in the opposite direction from the employee's office he disturbed a moment earlier.

CHAPTER 11

Like always, Aldo Brink had a plan. He arranged another meeting at the White House and he expected sparks to fly, unless of course he got what he wanted. If it worked, then everything would be fine. If not, he had something else up his sleeve. Just a few days after Jazlyn's arrest, he put something in motion that would ensure her freedom.

He ran into Chris Spencer, the head of the Presidential Security detail on his way in. Spencer had been trying to contact him for months, but Brink hadn't taken his calls. Brink laid out everything to him. He told him how his bosses were willing to sacrifice Jazlyn with altered evidence after looking the other way for years when it came to Thornburg. Spencer couldn't believe it. Brink said he understood, but gave him a warning as well. "Stay out of my way."

Chris Spencer, while not aware of Brink's full career, did have firsthand knowledge of his expertise in dealing with adversaries. He wasn't eager to be a name on that list. At that moment, Spencer became quite uneasy. Aldo Brink was the last man on Earth he wanted to be a threat, for a host of reasons, both personal and professional.

This time, not only didn't he wear a tie, Brink didn't even wear a suit. He wore dark blue jeans, tan boots, and a black button down shirt with the sleeves rolled up. When he walked in, Director Abraham pulled him aside to let him know it was unacceptable.

"We look the other way when you don't wear a tie, but today you just look like a slob. Wear a suit when you come to the White House," Abraham said.

"With everything going on, you come at me with a dress code violation?" Brink's voice dripped with disdain.

"Listen, I know you're going through a lot with all this…"

Brink stopped him cold. "You don't know anything; or maybe you do and you're part of the problem. Don, what do you know about what's going on here?"

"Leave it alone."

"You coward." Brink felt disgusted with his boss and disgusted with himself that he once respected the man. He knew more than he let on, Brink thought. His career had given him the opportunity to hone the skill of reading people. Brink had it down to a science. Abraham radiated shame, and even the old spymaster himself couldn't hide it.

President Richard Wilson entered the room followed by his Chief of Staff, and Deputy Director Sam Hodges. He motioned for them to have a seat.

"I'll stand," Brink said. Everyone else took a seat.

"Come on, sit down Aldo," Hodges said.

Brink was about to explode. "Are you deaf?"

The President tried to defuse the tension with some small talk which only made Brink angrier. An innocent woman's life hung in the balance and these guys were acting like nothing was going on.

"Mr. Brink," the President began. "You asked for this meeting and we are all here. What can we do for you?"

What do you think you can do for me? You know why I'm here.

"My fiancée has been charged with murder using false evidence, while the Vice President's drug use has been covered up."

The President didn't like this. "That's outrageous," the President said. "The investigation showed that she had cocaine in her system."

Brink bluffed.

"Save it. I know the cocaine is a lie. Jaz would never touch drugs. I also know drugs were found in both their systems, but it was GHB and not cocaine. Jazlyn received a much larger dose which would explain her confusion afterwards. What are they going to say next? That she tried to rape him with a date rape drug? Or maybe she drugged herself with a date rape drug? How come no vials or containers were found with her fingerprints on them? It had to have been stored in something."

"How did you come by this information?" asked Hodges.

"That's irrelevant. You know and I know it can't be proven in court. The bottom line is this, the bastard Vice President tried to rape my fiancée and you cowards are willing to sacrifice an innocent woman to protect the facade of your pathetic reputations. Am I getting warm, Dick?" No one called Richard Wilson, Dick.

The Chief of Staff leapt to his feet. "How dare you speak to the President in this fashion!" he said.

"Dick, tell your fat ass friend to shut his mouth before he gets hurt. He's just as responsible for this as the rest of you."

The President took a deep breath. "Mr. Brink, what is it that you want?"

"I want you and your band of merry men to concoct a story. I've seen you do it a hundred times so I know it's no big deal. The story can be anything you want as long as it results in all charges being dropped against Jazlyn Reyes. You will also direct the Attorney General to hold a press conference with Jazlyn with all the media in attendance, and he will make a personal apology in person to her on camera for putting her through this."

Everyone slumped back in their chairs. Brink continued, "Now you don't have to tell the truth about that son of a bitch Thornburg. Nominate him for the Nobel Prize for all I care, and if you can't come up with a suitable story to tell, then you can always just tell the truth and say the Vice President tried to rape her and she fought back. It might even help you with female voters!"

"Mr. Brink, you know we can't do that. The integrity of the administration must be protected," the President said.

"All I have done for this country and this is how you repay me? You people are a cancer on society. You promise hope to people who cry out for it, but you wouldn't know integrity if it smacked you in the face."

"Spare us the lecture," the Chief of Staff said.

Brink moved towards the President and took an aggressive posture. He looked like a caged lion that could rip a man to shreds in seconds once his paw slipped the latch on his temporary confinement. Abraham got worried at the sight of it. "Aldo, stop!" he said.

Brink's voice softened in volume, but rose in intensity. "This is your last chance. Right now, you can do the right thing."

"We can't do it." Brink didn't even know who said it, but he knew it wasn't the President since he was in his face, up close and personal.

"Then you all have a very large problem on your hands. I don't think you realize just how big yet, but you will. I promise you will. When it happens, just remember that you were the ones that started this, not me."

Brink turned and walked out of the Oval Office. The people he left didn't realize it yet, but Aldo Brink was at war.

CHAPTER 12

Gloria Smith stayed in town. She changed hotels a few times, but that was fine with her. She never liked to stay in one place for very long, both for security reasons and to satisfy her restless nature.

"You dumb bitch!" were the first words she heard upon answering the phone. Her employer's tone made his feelings clear. Furious didn't even begin to describe it. "Do you have any idea what you've done to us?" the voice on the phone asked.

"What are you talking about? The client's hands are clean and everything is working out perfectly," Gloria said. "The trial starts in a week and it's a slam dunk."

"You were supposed to act a week later and use someone of the client's choosing!"

"It was a perfect opportunity. I took the initiative." Gloria didn't know why, but she had this overwhelming feeling that she must have been missing something. Her snap decision had resulted in the perfect crime and no one suspected a thing. Besides the news reports on TV, the only theories resided in the usual arena of conspiracy kooks who were blaming everything from aliens to the ghost of Elvis. Yet, her employer sounded more upset with her than she'd ever heard him before.

"You just don't get it, you stupid fucking bitch!" the voice said.

"What don't I get? What aren't you telling me?"

The voice cleared his throat and took a deep breath. "Are you familiar with the name, Aldo Brink?"

Gloria stood up. Her heart rate quickened at the mere mention of his name. "Of course I do. Among our kind, he is the best there is." Though she had never met him, she had seen a photo headshot. He was just like her, she thought, ruthless and calculating. She knew about many of his past deeds, and felt a strong attraction to him as a result. If she could, she would love to kill with him forever.

The voice of her employer interrupted her daydream.

"Well, you dumb bitch. Jazlyn Reyes is Aldo Brink's fiancée." The voice let that sit out there for a moment before continuing. "Now do you see what the problem is?"

"Had I known, I wouldn't have…"

"Shut up, you fool. Your impulses got the better of you."

"I will take him out," she said. "With him out of the picture, the client should be covered."

"Are you out of your mind? He will see you coming a mile away, chop you up into little pieces, identify you, and then this whole damn thing will blow up in our faces! You say you've heard of him, so are you aware of what he's capable of?"

Gloria Smith bit her lip. "Yes, I am."

"You will be contacted in the future if a course of action is required. God help you if Brink finds out about you." The voice clicked away.

Gloria Smith's hands shook as she poured some vodka into a small glass. Her breathing was heavy as she heard the lock on her door opening. She tensed up with anticipation. Had Brink found her already? Was he going to shoot her in the head, or torture her for a week so she would give up her secrets? The horrifying outcome excited her.

The sight of her lover walking in genuinely disappointed her. She craved meeting a man like Aldo Brink, but she knew her desires would have to wait, for now.

Gloria's man saw her shaking as she held her glass. The ice chattered inside it. "What's wrong?" he asked.

"I got a call."

"And?"

Gloria took a drink. "My love, we have a serious problem."

CHAPTER 13

Jazlyn Reyes sat in her cramped cell at the Wilson Federal Prison Complex, staring straight ahead for what seemed like hours. After a few minutes, she stood and paced back and forth with what little room she had. If she stood in the center of her cell and extended her arms, she could almost touch both walls.

The cell had a sink that dispensed cold water, a toilet, and a cement slab with a thin mattress on top where she slept. Being maximum security, she had no windows to the outside. The cell door was solid steel with a small window to the cell block so guards could see inside. The door had a small slot that could be slid open from the outside where meals and mail were delivered.

She rarely saw the sun, and could only use the shower when the guards authorized her to do so. Normal shoes were forbidden. Paper feet coverings were all that was provided and they did little to blunt the cold concrete floor.

The leering looks from some of the guards made her uneasy, but she tried to block them out for her own sanity's sake.

When she first arrived at the prison, they placed her in the general population and not the maximum security wing. While her lawyer raised Hell over it, the prison officials insisted it had merely been a simple paperwork error. Normally, someone in Jazlyn's position would be automatically segregated for her own safety as inmates often target famous newcomers who they've seen on the news.

One day in the prison mess hall, a burly woman approached Jazlyn as she ate. "How ya doin, pretty girl?" she asked.

"I'm fine," Jazlyn said.

"The food ain't good enough for you I see. Well, I'm sure I can find you something to eat."

When the woman put her hand on Jazlyn's shoulder, she stood up to defend herself. Before she knew it, a mini riot had broken out with women fighting and throwing meal trays. Though outnumbered, Jazlyn got a few shots in, but ended up with a bruised cheek in the process. After a few days, prison officials sent her to a maximum security cell.

Though he couldn't prove it, Jazlyn's lawyer speculated that the whole fight might have been some kind of jailhouse intimidation that might lead to her accepting a guilty plea at trial. It seemed too coincidental with the paperwork error and all.

Jazlyn had been raised strict Catholic by her Brazilian immigrant parents. Both of them told her stories about how their faith in God had sustained them during the hardships imposed in their native land, and how their faith protected them as they made the dangerous journey to America. After her father had prospered as a restaurant owner in Miami, he would always give thanks to God and America, in that order, for making it possible.

Admittedly, Jazlyn had not been to church or prayed in a very long time. She still believed in God, but her fast pace lifestyle and her career had left little time for anything else. The thing about confinement of this nature is that it gives you lots of time to think, and forces you to do so since you can't do anything else. Jazlyn found this out firsthand.

Now, Jazlyn prayed for answers. Had she done something to deserve this? Was she being punished for some action or inaction on her part? She begged God to help her somehow and apologized for not going to church in years, knowing full well that God would never punish her like this for such a small infraction. People all over the world didn't go to church regularly and they weren't imprisoned in a hellhole for it. Still, Jazlyn reached for anything in order to explain her situation, and was willing to at least entertain any possibility, spiritual or not.

All she did was go to a party, felt dizzy, and the next thing she knew she had a man's hands around her throat. Getting her day in court gave her no hope. The deck had been stacked against her from day one. Aldo made sure she had the best lawyer, but it wasn't going to be enough. She dreaded the thought of her fiancé and all he must be feeling. Aldo was the type of guy who always put on a brave face for her, but she knew he must be struggling on the inside. He talked to her parents and tried to reassure them, while she felt too ashamed to even see them.

One evening, she just cried and cried as she tried to get comfortable on the concrete slab they called a bed. Feeling sorry for herself wasn't going to improve her situation, but everything just felt hopeless.

"Please rescue me from this Hell," she said, hoping someone up there would answer her cries for help.

CHAPTER 14

After storming out of the White House, Brink needed to clear his head. Once he retrieved the Glock from his BMW, he decided to take a walk downtown. The majesty of the Lincoln Memorial didn't quite have the same honor to it as it did a few months ago. Brink had been around the block, and the irony hadn't been lost on him. He had dedicated his life to defending America by any means necessary. Often, that resulted in breaking the law and doing things many people would consider intolerable. Now, he found himself on a collision course with people who said they were doing essentially the same thing.

Brink didn't buy it. The people allowing Jazlyn to waste away in prison were not doing it to protect the American people. They were doing it to protect themselves. They were selfish, had an unquenchable thirst for power, and they didn't care who they hurt in order to keep it. They thought they were bigger than the system. The same system he bled to protect.

Brink thought everything through. If these people in the Oval Office were willing to let Jazlyn rot in prison for life, or be condemned to the death penalty, why wouldn't they just kill her now and prevent her self-defense argument from even being argued in court? That way their cover story would hold. They would make it look like a suicide and no one would care about a dead junkie who murdered the Vice President. It would be on the news for a few days, and then it would be over.

He didn't know if that was their plan, but either way he wasn't going to wait around to find out. They had declared war on him by involving Jazlyn in this. They probably didn't mean to since they wouldn't have wanted Aldo Brink as an enemy, but that didn't matter now.

The path Brink took would lead to people dying, and he didn't care. People would howl about innocent life being lost, but the way he saw it, Jazlyn was innocent too and no one seemed to care about her. If they wanted a free for all, he would oblige. Once Brink had freed his fiancée, they would have to go somewhere else for a long time, if not forever. The powers that be would never be able to prove officially that he had anything to do with her escape, but the power players who treated him like crap in the Oval Office would certainly know. He would make sure of it. He wanted them to know.

If they were smart, they would simply feign a manhunt for her for appearance sake, and let her and Brink live abroad in peace. The administration's lies would persist, and their story about Thornburg and how he died would be written in the history books. Why would they risk more of Brink's wrath by coming after them?

As he turned right and walked north up 23rd Street, Brink noticed a man following him. He was white, average height and build, and wearing a Washington Nationals baseball cap. Brink stopped for a moment and pretended to look at something across the street. While other pedestrians passed him or closed the distance, the man stopped as well and maintained his interval. Brink started walking, and the man followed.

When he came to Constitution Avenue, Brink turned right and led the man all the way to 17th Street. The man maintained his distance and followed him when he turned left and headed to G Street where he parked his BMW in the garage earlier.

Brink parked on the third level, and normally would use the stairs since he liked the exercise. This time he went to the elevator. As he hit the button, he saw the man coming up behind him in the reflection of the shiny elevator door.

The door opened and a young woman with two children walked out. Brink smiled and nodded at them, then entered. The man followed and stood to Brink's left. As the elevator door closed, he smiled and nodded in Brink's direction.

"How's it going?" the man asked.

"Good, thanks."

A split second before the elevator door closed, Brink unleashed a devastating kick to the man's right knee. The man fell and reached for his right hip. As he grabbed the handle of his pistol, Brink spun and connected with an elbow to the man's jaw, disorienting him. Brink moved behind the stranger and wrapped his arm around the man's neck, cutting his air supply. Just before the man passed out, Brink eased his grip. The elevator bell rung as they reached the third floor.

As he dragged the half unconscious man to his car, Brink clicked his remote trunk release. He took the man's pistol, tossed him in the trunk, and grabbed something from inside a small case. He snapped it off in front of the man's nose, instantly bringing him around.

"As you can see, the trunk is lined with plastic, so think about what you're going to tell me when I ask you a question."

The man nodded.

"Who are you and why are you following me?"

"ID is inside my jacket pocket."

Brink pointed the pistol at the man's head. "Take it out and hand it to me, slowly."

The man complied. His ID was similar to Brink's. It was a standard issue CIA Identity card used to pass through the turnstiles and enter the offices at Langley. It identified the man as Trent Richards.

"Do you know who I am?" Brink asked.

"I was told you were an agent the company feared was losing it. I was told to follow you and report if you did anything crazy."

"When were you ordered to do this?"

"Yesterday, they said to pick up your trail as you left the White House today."

"You have no idea what they've thrust you into. You have a phone?" Brink asked. The man nodded and pulled it from his pocket. "Dial Sam Hodges, and put it on speaker."

The man gave a shrug to indicate he had no idea how to contact the deputy director.

"Dial the number in five seconds or I'm going to cut your eyes out." Brink didn't even have to produce a knife to show he wasn't bluffing. In seconds the phone started to ring, and seconds later Sam Hodges answered.

"Agent Richards, report."

"Tell him where you are," Brink said as he gestured to his captive in the trunk.

"I'm in his trunk, sir. It's lined with plastic and he's pointing my gun at me."

"Brink, release him this instant," Hodges said. "I just told him to follow you, because we are worried about you."

"Worried about me? How do I know you didn't send him to kill me? Were you sent to kill me, Agent Richards?" Brink pushed the pistol into his captive's cheek. Richards winced in pain.

"You're not helping her by doing this," Hodges said. "Brink, stop this! Whatever you think you can do, just stop thinking about it. You can't save her. That ship has sailed. There is nothing anyone can do."

"We'll see." Brink hung up the phone and tossed it away. He motioned for his captive to get out of the trunk. Richards quickly obeyed. Brink racked the slide back and forth until Richards' pistol had no ammunition, ejected the magazine, and tossed the pistol down the ramp to the second level of the garage.

"Is this about a woman?" Richards asked. Brink could tell it wasn't an act. The man had no idea what this was about.

"If I see you again, I'll kill you."

Brink closed the trunk, got behind the wheel, and slammed the car into reverse. He would have run Trent Richards over if he hadn't crawled out of the way just in time.

Ready to act, Aldo Brink drove south. When he turned onto Interstate 66 and headed west, he was more than willing for that to be the last time he ever set foot in the nation's capital. Innocent people were going to die soon, but Brink took no responsibility for that. He didn't set this in motion. They did. He didn't ask for this. He never wanted this. They declared war on his only family. If his adversaries had no regard for the innocent, then he wouldn't either. If anyone got in his way, they would be eliminated.

Before every operation he wondered if all the planning and risk were worth the future result. In this case, he didn't even have to think about it. To him, Jazlyn was worth everything.

His capabilities were beyond their comprehension. Sure, they knew he was a serious man, but they also thought they could stop him if it came to that. As he drove along the interstate and further away from his home that he would never see again, a devilish smile graced his face.

They aren't going to know what hit them.

CHAPTER 15

The trial started in two days. It would be agonizing for Jazlyn and her family. The outcome was never in doubt. Legal experts on television never even argued her innocence or guilt. They discussed whether she would rot in prison for life, or be put to death by lethal injection after being on Death Row for a few years first. Brink couldn't stop the trial, but he would make damn sure Jazlyn Reyes would be tried in absentia.

Once the trial began, Jazlyn would be transferred to a facility closer to the courthouse. Brink knew this would make her extraction more difficult. If given the choice, he would much rather attack a rural target, and that is exactly what the Wilson Federal Prison Complex was. The prison, located approximately 175 miles from downtown Washington near the town of Farmville, was ironically named after President Richard Wilson, who while serving as the Governor of Virginia, signed a sweeping prison bill boondoggle that ushered in its construction. The voters praised him for being tough on crime, but truthfully it was nothing more than a giant kickback to some of his political donors who were rewarded with hundreds of millions in "no bid" contracts.

At 2 AM, Aldo Brink watched at exactly 300 yards from the Wilson Federal Prison Complex where his fiancée sat locked in a cell. He lay in a prone position, dressed from head to toe in black. The level IV ballistic armor he wore made him more bulky than he preferred, but while speed was critical, brute force and precision were what would pull this off. He didn't have far to go. Once the wall was breached, he would sprint 300 yards and enter the complex, taking out the two guard towers along the way. From there, he estimated it would be another 175 yards to Jazlyn's cell. *I'm coming, Jaz.*

The sky was overcast, and as a result the lack of moonlight helped conceal his position. He lay just outside the area where the groundskeepers kept the grass short. The unruly weeds that Brink surrounded himself with meant none of the guards in the watch towers could see him. Brink didn't feel bad for what was about to happen to them. Soon, they would be dead. Some by his hand, some not, but by his doing just the same. Their families shouldn't blame him, he thought. They should blame the people at 1600 Pennsylvania Avenue.

No matter, though. He wasn't trying to win a popularity contest or man of the year. His goal was to rescue the woman he loved by any means necessary. He had considered a less aggressive approach where he would minimize the loss of life, if not rule it out altogether, but that approach would increase the risk of failure and he wasn't prepared to accept that. He knew the second he breached those walls, the guards inside would try to kill him. They wouldn't ask why he was doing this, nor would they care about the truth behind Jazlyn's incarceration. They would draw their guns, and shoot to kill. He would do the same.

Brink could have done it alone and had contingencies for that approach, but if he wanted to give himself as close to a one hundred percent chance of success as possible, he needed some extra equipment and resources.

Having almost as many false identities as the President had mistresses made getting out of the country unnoticed simple. A decade ago, Brink came to the conclusion that having false identities and bank accounts belonging to them for a rainy day that no one at Langley knew about was a prudent way to protect his own life, and future.

His rainy day plans would be put to good use, just not for the reason he originally intended.

Only a few days after Jazlyn's arrest, Brink hopped a commercial flight to India under the name Tracy Harlem, aluminum salesman. Though it didn't have the same ring to it as "Bond, James Bond," he always thought the name belonged on a soap opera. Just in case the powers that be were monitoring his face, he wore faux facial hair, colored contacts, eyeglasses, and a set of false teeth inserts that made him particularly hard to look at.

After landing at Dabolim Airport, Brink took a taxi north across the Zuari River. He continued along the coast until he reached Panaji, one of the wealthiest cities in India in per capita terms. Hotels filled the coastline. Tourism in India had skyrocketed over the past decade. Their economy was growing and they boasted the second highest number of English language speakers after the United States. White English speaking tourists could be found all over the country so fitting in later wouldn't be a problem. Though many spoke the English language, Hindi was the language most spoken and sadly Brink didn't speak a word of it. It was one of the most pro-American countries in the world and public polling showed that the average citizen in India held a higher favorable opinion of the USA than even their longtime ally the British.

The man he journeyed to see had a lot to do with India's rapid rise to world power. Their economy grew by leaps and bounds, bringing people out of poverty, and they owed it to men like Soham Gupta. Born in the slums of Mumbai, Gupta and his family struggled for everything. Today, Mumbai boasted a growing prosperous middle class, but huge sections of the city were still poverty stricken. When Soham was born, there was almost no middle class to speak of.

He had come a long way from those days. Today, he owned four homes in India alone, as well as villas in London, Rome, and Los Angeles. The Los Angeles

Hollywood Hills residence was more for his daughter than himself. She dreamed of becoming an international actress and working with Hollywood's leading men.

Soham Gupta rose to become the manufacturing king of Asia. While China dominated the headlines for the massive volume of products they produced for the West, Gupta's companies took a different approach. They focused on quality over quantity, and by doing so had built themselves an internationally respected brand.

Soham had worked in the rat-infested factories of the past where workers committed suicide due to the abysmal working conditions, and he made sure that would never happen in one of his factories. Every time Brink saw him, he was always impeccably dressed in either the finest European or Indian styled clothing, but once a week he went to a different factory and physically worked on the assembly line for eight hours with his employees. He was a billionaire many times over, but the people of India saw him as a member of their family due to his many acts of generosity.

Brink couldn't help but compare him to former Vice President Thornburg who was born with all the advantages in the world, yet turned into nothing but a lazy womanizing drunk. Soham Gupta had to eat out of the trash as a boy, yet made himself into a national hero who helped people with his hard earned money.

He became a national hero in his country for providing so many people safe well-paying jobs. He was so well regarded that his endorsement during the last round of elections had catapulted the current Prime Minister into his new post thanks to massive public support for his party after Soham Gupta held a press conference with him. He had been urged to seek political office on numerous occasions, but he always politely declined. His name Gupta, was derived from "goptri" which meant ruler or protector. Soham said he never wanted to rule over anyone, but he did want to protect his people.

Brink knew that Soham spent every spring here at his coastal estate in Panaji. As the taxi pulled away, he removed his facial alterations and put them in his duffel bag. Brink reached the massive gate at the driveway, and rang the doorbell.

"Welcome to the Gupta Estate. How may we help you?" the voice said from the speaker.

"Good afternoon. My name is Aldo Brink and I am here to see Mr. Gupta. He is expecting me."

"Mr. Brink, welcome. We were expecting you. I guessed that it was you and decided to practice my English. How am I doing with it?"

"Fantastic, Raj. You really have improved," Brink said, realizing he was talking to Soham's longtime butler.

After being buzzed in, he ascended the countless steps of the majestic estate. At the top he saw his old friend waiting for him. Soham bounded down the steps and met Brink half way. He put his hands together and greeted Brink with the Namaste, a traditional Indian greeting.

"Welcome my friend. I insist on carrying your bag. You will stay with me here for as long as you like." Soham snatched Brink's duffel bag away from him and they walked up the stairs together. At the top, Soham's servants were waiting with drinks and appetizers.

"Soham, you didn't have to do all this for me."

"Nonsense, without you, my life would be nothing."

Seeing how much it meant to the man, Brink accepted his hospitality and after listening to Soham's toast, took a drink.

"Soham, I need to speak with you in private right away." Upon hearing this, Soham waved off his staff. Soham led Brink to a secluded balcony that overlooked the water. The view was outstanding.

"What is it that has caused you to travel so far to see me? Something must be troubling you. Is it a health issue? I will have the best doctors in the world here in 48 hours."

"No, no, it's nothing like that."

"Whatever it is, tell me and I will help you," Soham said.

"I need to ask you a favor. It's a lot to ask and you know I would never come to you like this unless it was serious."

"Yes, of course I know this. I have offered you things for years and you never accept anything. I will never forget what you did for me. I owe you everything. Tell me what is going on."

"I assume you know about the Vice President who was killed?"

"Yes, of course. He was killed by a woman. He was a dreadful man though, I must say."

"You don't know this, but he was killed by a woman in self-defense. He was trying to rape her. They are going to put her away for life, or worse, based on lies."

"Oh my God, Aldo how do you know this?" Soham asked.

"She is my fiancée." Soham walked away a few steps, then returned and put his arm around his friend.

"Aldo, this saddens me deeply. I can't imagine your pain. What can I do? Name it."

"Soham, I need some money to help her," Brink said.

"You will have all the money you need. She will have the best legal defense."

Brink shook his head. "No Soham, the money is not for a legal defense."

"Then what is it for?"

"It's for breaking her out and giving her a new life. I will have to kill people to do it." Soham waited a few seconds to understand the implications. He had never been involved in anything nefarious. His business practices were all above board, and he had never hurt a soul. Could he live with helping Aldo Brink kill people who may or not deserve to die?

"You will have fifty million US dollars in untraceable funds. I assume you still have some front companies that no one knows about where I can discreetly transfer the money to. Or would you prefer cash flown to a place of your choosing by one of my trusted pilots?"

"I don't deserve your generosity," Brink said.

"You and I both know that's not true."

"I can't accept so much from you. I had a much smaller amount in mind."

"You can, and you will accept it. The discussion on this issue is over," Soham said.

Had Soham been unable or unwilling to help, Brink had other plans that he was confident he could pull off. This would make things easier, though. He thanked Soham for his generosity as he felt a tug on his shoulder.

When he turned around, he was greeted by a beautiful young woman. Though he hadn't seen her in five years, her face could only be that of Priyanka Gupta, Soham's daughter and only child. Kavitha, Priyanka's mother, had died in a car accident when she was only ten. After that, the bond between father and daughter deepened significantly. Soham's handsome face and wealth placed him at the top of India's most eligible bachelor list every year, but he never even looked at another woman. His heart still belonged to his deceased wife. While heartbroken with the loss of his soul mate, the love for Priyanka kept him going.

"I bet your father has to hire special security to keep the boys away," Brink said.

"He tries!" Priyanka said as she jumped into Brink's arms.

As Soham saw his daughter's beautiful smile as she embraced Aldo, he knew he made the right decision to help him. Whatever the financial or moral costs, they were worth it. It was only five years ago that his only child was almost taken from him and he had not forgotten the feeling he had when he thought she was gone forever, thrust into Hell.

His daughter was sixteen and on holiday with some friends in Prague. Soham knew he shouldn't have let her go but he wanted to make his daughter happy, so in the end he relented to her wishes.

She was having fun in one of the clubs downtown when she vanished. The authorities were incompetent or corrupt, and there seemed to be no hope in recovering her unharmed. Little did Soham know at the time, but Aldo Brink was deep undercover and on the trail of the human traffickers who had kidnapped his daughter and planned to sell her into sexual slavery to a host of unsavory characters in the Middle East.

While trailing the leader of the group, Brink faced a decision. With his target heading one way, and an innocent girl being moved another way, his orders were to stay with the leader and let the girl go. His superiors felt the greater good was to kill or capture the leader, thus saving countless girls in the future.

Brink saw an innocent girl who would be lost forever right in front of him. She would be drugged and used as a prostitute for sickos in the Middle East who were buying her in a fashion reminiscent of 18th century slavery.

Aldo Brink broke off the chase for his target, killed her captors before they could deliver her to the buyer, and rescued Priyanka Gupta. After her rescue, Priyanka heard the radio communication between Brink and his superiors. She heard how he had come back for her, and she heard his superiors chew him out. He didn't know her. She was a complete stranger, but he had come back for her. A few days later, Brink showed up in Panaji and delivered Priyanka Gupta to her father whose happiness rendered him unable to speak.

When she told her father about all of this, he promised Brink anything he wanted. As a billionaire, he was one of the few people who could actually deliver on such a promise. Had it not been for Aldo Brink, his daughter would be dead or condemned to a horrific life of hellish torture. Fifty million dollars meant nothing compared to what Brink had delivered to him five years ago. Thinking back, if Soham had to kill to get his daughter back, he would have.

"You will have what you need, and then some," Soham said, as he wrapped his arms around Brink and his daughter. "I know what you're feeling, Aldo. I want you to get her back, by any means necessary."

Brink stayed the night and made arrangements with Soham for the money, but he still needed more help and some major firepower. By next afternoon, he was on his way to get it.

CHAPTER 16

Rodney and Hakim Harrison were happy to be in Mauritius. They had arrived in the beautiful island nation yesterday and were planning to meet an old friend of theirs in Port Louis, the capital city. It had been two years since they last saw their friend, but they had stayed in touch through discreet channels.

The Harrison brothers had become quite the entrepreneurs. They owned a bit of real estate that generated a decent income. They also took the occasional contract when they thought the money was right, and the motive righteous.

Brink had sent them a coded message to meet at a waterside café they were all familiar with. Rodney, the more serious of the two, sat relaxed, yet extremely alert. They weren't being hunted by anyone they knew of and weren't on any watch lists or fugitive rosters. The only people that would have cared about them were at Langley, and thanks to Aldo Brink, they were under the impression that the Harrison brothers died in a Bolivian torture chamber.

Brink came walking down the sidewalk only a few minutes after Rodney sat down at a secluded table outside. Brink sat down across from his old friend.

"Hakim?"

"He's just checking things out, making sure we're all clear. He'll be here any second."

"Good," Brink said. "I've been looking forward to seeing you both."

"So what's this about, man? I'm happy to see you, but I can't help but think the shit has really hit the fan if you were willing to come all this way after two years."

"I need your help."

"With what?" Rodney asked. A waiter arrived at the table and poured two glasses of water.

"Make it three, my man," Hakim said as he strolled to the table while holding up three fingers, unsure if the waiter spoke English. Hakim sat down and tapped Brink on the chest. "How've you been, man?"

"That's why I'm here, Hakim," Brink said. "I'm not doing so well. I need your help."

"Whatever you need man, we got your back," Hakim said.

"Let's see what he wants first," Rodney said.

Hakim didn't like his older brother's tone, and turned to Brink. "Man, forget him; I'm rolling with you, point blank."

"It's OK, Rodney is just being smart," Brink said. "You guys heard about the Vice President being killed by that woman, right?"

"Yeah, he was an asshole," Hakim said.

"The woman is my fiancée."

Brink told them the whole story. Both brothers were quite upset upon hearing what had happened to the woman Aldo Brink planned to marry. While Rodney could always keep a lid on his emotions just like his father, Hakim took after his mother and wore his emotions on his sleeve.

"I'll kill all those sons of bitches!" Hakim said as he slammed his mammoth fist down onto the table.

Rodney never liked these emotional outbursts from his little brother. "Chill, brother. We'll work it out."

"We better, cuz this shit ain't gonna stand! On mom and dad's graves, this shit ain't gonna stand!"

Rodney and Hakim had no respect for authority after their years of field work. They were treated like pawns on a chess board and had felt for years that if they were considered pawns by others, then they would treat others the same way. That's just how the world worked, they concluded, and they weren't going to fight it anymore.

They might have been noble once, but not anymore. After Bolivia, Rodney and Hakim tracked down the support team member of the no name unit who burned them. It turned out that it wasn't one person at all, but a husband and wife team that were new to the unit. They were promoted from the clandestine service and had extensive experience in South American operations. The

Harrison brothers not only killed him, but they killed his wife, too. A quick bullet to their heads was their idea of mercy given what Alejandro Alvarez was going to do to them in Bolivia. They let the dog and the infant son live. Aldo Brink was the only reason the Harrison brothers were still alive today, and they hadn't forgotten what he did for them.

"We're in. So what are you thinking?" Rodney asked.

"I want to send a message," Brink said.

"Hell yeah! Let's make it loud and clear to those bastards that they fucked with the wrong woman," Hakim said. His fury seemed to grow by the second. "We still have some serious shit stored away. You remember it, right? We got about 1.9 mill in cash stored with it."

"You never dipped into that money?"

"Hell no. It was all of ours. We didn't think it was right to spend it until we talked to you."

"Well, split it between the two of you. It's all yours. I've been able to make arrangements for funding the op and my future with Jazlyn," Brink said.

"So what's the plan?" asked Rodney.

Brink took a long drink of water. "Jericho, with a twist."

"Jericho with a twist!" Hakim said. "Let's do it."

"I'm in too," Rodney said.

"Thanks, fellas. I assume the *big* stash is in the same place we left it. You didn't move it, did you?"

"It's still there. I checked it two months ago. Everything is in working order."

"You were in town Rodney, and you didn't say hi?"

The men chuckled and bumped their water glasses together. "I know this makes me a bad person, but I'm going to enjoy this," Hakim said.

Brink slid a small piece of paper across the table to Rodney. "Meet at the stash then. You can man it yourselves, right?"

"Absolutely," Hakim said.

"See you then." Brink got up and walked away. He disappeared out of sight in less than sixty seconds.

Hakim turned back to his older brother. "It's on."

They won't know what hit them.

CHAPTER 17

About a month later Brink rendezvoused with the Harrison brothers in rural Virginia, about 90 miles from the prison where the love of his life was being held. Many years ago Brink had the idea to buy some property under a false name and store some equipment there. Essentially, it was their rainy day fund, and Rodney Harrison was the trustee. He stocked it, monitored it, and decided what should be sold or bartered if they needed to raise cash or buy new equipment.

The old industrial property was perfect. It was in the middle of nowhere with only a single dirt road giving access. The trees surrounding it provided additional cover. Brink found the place and Rodney was put in charge of renovating it. He fortified the main building, and basically turned a portion of it into a secure storage facility.

Inside the facility were enough weapons and munitions to re-launch the Bay of Pigs, except this time, it would work. Military grade rifles of various types, pistols, explosives, body armor, and enough ammunition to invade a small country were organized and ready to go at a moment's notice. Behind the weapons were three vehicles.

The first was a Robinson R66 single rotor five seat helicopter that Rodney had painted black. It cruised at about 130 MPH with a range of 375 miles. It was small, had no weapons, and couldn't carry much, but for ferrying people quickly, it was perfect. While much of the gear was stolen or purchased on the black market, the R66 was bought legally from the manufacturer with cash for $850,000.

The second was the massive HET, or Heavy Equipment Transporter. It was a semi-truck on steroids with a massive trailer behind it. It was used to transport tanks and other heavy vehicles to and from the battlefield. Brink and the Harrison brothers stole it and its cargo from an Army base in upstate New York six years ago. They figured they might need it one day for one of their operations. The Army played it off as a mere clerical error. It wasn't stolen because it never existed in the first place, they said.

The third vehicle was the cargo the HET was hauling on the day they stole it. The M270 MLRS, or Multiple Launch Rocket System, was a Cold War era weapon that had been upgraded over the years to carry smart precision guided missiles. It could fire surface to surface missiles from over 100 miles away with devastating accuracy or a variety of other munitions. This unit however was fitted with two MGM-140 Army Tactical Missiles.

Once the plan was set, Rodney rented a tanker truck and made sure all the vehicles were topped off with fuel.

Operation Jericho was a World War II bombing raid by Allied aircraft on Amiens Prison in German occupied France on February 18, 1944. The raid was designed to free political prisoners by bombing the walls of the prison thereby causing a jail break. Of the 717 prisoners, 102 were killed, 74 were wounded, and 258 escaped, including 79 resistance and political prisoners, although two thirds of the escapees were recaptured. Brink planned to be more precise. That's where the twist came in.

The three men had pulled a Jericho before to free prisoners and cause chaos, but this time they had to be sure they weren't dropping a bomb on Jazlyn's head by accident. Finding out where she was in the prison was easy, but the rest would require perfect timing. Rodney Harrison wasn't in the same league with Taylor Ross, but hacking the federal prison system to find out which cell Jazlyn resided in was something he handled with little difficulty.

Hakim was so amped up he wanted to steal an AC-130 Spectre gunship from a military base and use that to pull the Jericho, but Rodney and Brink eventually talked him down and convinced him that they had a better plan.

As Brink lay in the tall grass observing the prison with his night vision scope, he calmly looked at his watch and knew that Rodney and Hakim had set the plan in motion. There was no going back now. He thought to himself about what Hakim had said to him so many times just prior to an operation going hot.

"It's on."

CHAPTER 18

Brink waited patiently. The time indicated that Hakim had already launched two hellacious missiles that were streaking their way to their targets at supersonic speeds. He had simply driven the vehicle outside from their hangar and launched the missiles from their very own property. After a bit of time, it wouldn't be too difficult to track down where the launch location was, so the minute they were launched, Hakim drove away in his rented car. They had thought about trying to keep the MLRS, but it was just too risky. Abandoning it made their escape easier, and Brink reimbursed the Harrison brothers for the $2,000,000 cost of the vehicle anyway.

Checking his watch again, Brink knew time was short. At 90 miles away, the missiles would have a flight time of less than six minutes, which meant in approximately thirty seconds all Hell would break loose. Brink reached to his side and grabbed his mask. He put it on and adjusted it. His chiseled handsome face had been replaced with a horrific yellow Halloween skull mask that completely covered his head and face from front to back. Only his eyes were visible. If the explosions and gunfire weren't enough, seeing a yellow skull coming through the smoke would unnerve anyone who saw him, giving him an edge. Plus, he just liked the look of it.

The first missile slammed into the outer prison wall right on schedule. For a brief moment, the pitch black night was illuminated with a brilliant flash. Brink could hear the cement and steel fall like toothpicks under the tremendous force they had just come in contact with. While his adrenalin surged, he remained calm and waited a beat, just in time to see the second missile obliterate the inner wall of the prison that led directly to the cell block where Jazlyn resided.

Brink rose to his feet and sprinted forward towards the massive breach in the prison wall. He wasn't moving as fast as he wanted. He was weighed down with his M249 PARA Light Machine Gun slung over his back, two M72 LAW rockets, and a duffel bag with explosives. He also carried an HK45 pistol loaded with hollow point ammunition. As he reached his first mark, Brink heard the alarms sound inside the prison. While he planned the attack, he had thought about cutting the power, but he wanted the security cameras to keep recording. He wanted *them* to see what he had done.

He lightened his load when he stopped 100 yards from the wall. He brought one of the LAW rockets to his shoulder, aimed, and fired the weapon at the guard tower on the left. He couldn't tell if anyone was in the tower at the time, but he didn't care either way. The towers were no threat as he was coming in, but they had the potential to harass them going out. As the rocket exploded on impact, Brink dropped his empty launcher and shouldered the next one. He aimed right, took a breath, and fired.

As the towers smoldered, Brink was on the run again towards the wall. The smoke made it difficult to see as he reached it. He climbed up the two foot high rubble of the wall. The missile had done a wonderful job by turning much of the cement to dust, but the debris was still considerable. Brink made a mental note to give extra help to Jazlyn as they traversed it on the way out. He didn't want her twisting an ankle on the uneven debris.

The inside of the prison yard was illuminated with bright flood lights as the alarm continued to blare. Reinforcements would arrive at the prison soon, but they were of no concern. By the time they arrived, Brink and Jazlyn would be long gone. Brink brought his M249 around to the front of his body as he continued to the second wall's breach point.

He could see some guards running around in the adjacent buildings, but nobody had seen him yet. Just as Brink suspected, everyone was so shocked at what was happening that chaos had erupted among the prison staff. Their protocols had kicked in which required an immediate lockdown of the entire prison and for the guards to take up an aggressive anti-riot stance. They were probably grabbing their riot shields and putting on body armor this very minute, Brink thought. As he got closer, Brink reached into his duffel bag and placed a few small mines where he thought guards might try to flank him once he breached the cell block. If he heard them explode, he would know they were coming, but if even one went off it would undoubtedly scare the Hell out of the remaining guards and could perhaps even force them to turn back.

Brink jumped over the debris at the base of the breach in the wall. The cell block was illuminated, and as he came around the corner two guards turned around and saw him. They were thirty feet away and it looked like they were checking the cell block's integrity after the explosions. The look on their face as they saw the yellow skull faced man walk toward them was something Brink had seen many times before. He knew that most people reacted slowly under stress and these men were no different as they drew their guns.

"Raise those guns and you die!" Brink growled.

Had they dropped their guns and run away, Brink would have let them go, but when they raised their pistols, he opened fire. From about twenty feet away, his M249 ripped them both to shreds before they could even fire a shot. Brink ran past them, passing Jazlyn's cell as he reached the end of the hall where he made sure the cell block gate was locked and secure. He pulled a Claymore mine from his small duffel bag and attached it to the wall next to the gate using the double sided adhesive tape he had lined it with earlier. If anyone made it through that gate, they would be met with the explosive force of the Claymore.

Brink ran to Jazlyn's cell and peered in the narrow window. She was there. She was five feet away, standing in the middle of her cell looking confused. She was no doubt awakened by all the noise, but had no idea what was going on. Brink yelled for his fiancée.

"Jazlyn!"

Upon seeing the freakish mask through the window, Jazlyn took a step back. Brink drew his pistol and shot the security camera pointed at him, then pulled off his mask revealing the face that Jazlyn had fallen in love with. Her eyes got wide as she spoke, but couldn't muster any sound as she mouthed the name of her fiancé.

"Aldo."

"Jaz, I'm going to slip you a bomb blanket and ear plugs through the slot here. I'm going to breach the door, and the blanket will shield you from the debris. Put the ear plugs in, go to the far side of the cell in the corner and put your mattress up against the wall. Then cover yourself with the blanket and cover your ears with your hands. Do you understand me?"

Jazlyn quickly nodded yes.

Brink yanked the bomb blanket from his duffel bag, and then tossed the bag aside. He opened the slot in the door used for mail and food delivery and fed the blanket through. Jazlyn helped by yanking it through on her side. When she had it, Brink put his hand through the slot and handed her the ear plugs. Though he was wearing tactical gloves, he loved touching her hand again.

"OK, I'm setting the charges. I'm going to secure the door so it doesn't blow toward you. Get in the corner and cover yourself. Do it now!"

Brink took a long steel cable that was looped from his belt. He secured one end to the cell door and the other end to the cell door directly across from Jazlyn's. He checked left, and then right as he attached the breaching charges to the hinges. He had thought about attaching a charge to the deadbolt area as well, but he wanted the deadbolt to absorb some of the energy when the charges blew.

"We got a fire in the towers. We got guys burning alive up there!" Brink could hear from the dead guard's radio. There was screaming from outside, as they assessed the carnage.

Brink attached the detonator and moved to a safe distance. He dreaded this part the most. He was terrified of having the door blow in towards Jazlyn. If it hit her, she would be killed. When he detonated the charge, his plan worked perfectly. The cable held and absorbed a tremendous amount of energy as the explosion nearly pulled the other cell door off its hinges as well.

Brink pulled the cable with all his might. The cell door came crashing to the floor. As he looked inside the cell he saw that some minor debris and concrete dust covered the bomb blanket. Brink raced inside, yanked the blanket off and grabbed Jazlyn's hand pulling her up off the floor. He didn't worry about leaving any evidence behind. He handled everything with gloves so there would be no fingerprints.

"Can you move?"

"Yes," Jazlyn said, as she fought back tears, overwhelmed with the gravity of the moment.

"Stay close to me. You're getting out of here." Brink replaced his mask, raised his machine gun, and led her out the way he came. "Follow right behind me. I mined the way out."

"OK," Jazlyn said.

Brink led her through the smoke. When they cleared it, Brink opened fire on three guards who had taken a position outside. Positioning himself in front of Jazlyn, and acting as a human shield, he sent a volley of around 60 rounds towards their position. The M249 held a 200 round ammunition feed, and by Brink's rough estimate he had about 120 rounds left after his latest barrage. His suppressing fire caused the men to take cover, and then run left, just as Brink wanted. They had no idea they were running right into the mine field that Brink had laid minutes earlier.

The first two men were blown apart by the anti-personal mines, while the third tried to dive for cover. He probably saved his life by doing so, but was knocked out cold by the concussive force of the blasts.

As they ran to the breach in the outer wall, a guard came around the corner of the building that Brink had used for cover on the way in. He grabbed Brink from his right side and tried to snatch his gun away from him. The struggle lasted only five or six seconds as Brink ended it quickly with a knife thrust to the back of the man's neck.

In the commotion, Jazlyn had run ahead to the breach in the wall. Brink ran to catch up. They were almost there.

As Jazlyn reached the smoke at the base of the breached wall, a guard emerged from it and grabbed her. He spun her around, put his arm around her neck, and began to choke her.

Brink slung his M249 again, and drew his pistol. As he aimed his weapon from thirty feet away he recognized the guard. It was the same man who had been rough with Jazlyn as he removed her from the visiting chamber when Brink had come to see her. Brink pulled the hammer back on his HK45, giving the weapon a lighter trigger pull. He held his breath, and squeezed the trigger.

The .45 ACP hollow point bullet whizzed past Jazlyn's head at over 1000 feet per second and struck the guard an inch above his right eye. After the initial penetration, the bullet expanded inside the man's skull, just before he fell to the ground.

Brink ran forward, grabbed Jazlyn by the hand, and led her through the smoke. He got behind her and helped her up over the debris, and down the other side.

"Run!" Brink shouted, as a Robinson R66 helicopter touched down fifty yards in front of them. They were twenty-five yards from it when Jazlyn tripped. Brink reached down and lifted her to her feet once more as they sprinted towards the helicopter. Brink opened the door to the back seat of the R66 and helped Jazlyn inside. He checked their six, saw no one in pursuit, and boarded the chopper.

Rodney Harrison increased the throttle and gained as much altitude as he could before pointing the nose of the chopper downward generating as much speed as possible. Before long they had leveled out at 5,000 feet and were cruising towards Farmville Municipal Airport at 130 MPH.

Brink removed his mask, stuffed it into his pocket, and checked to make sure they weren't taking any incoming fire. "We're clear," he said. "Perfect timing, my friend."

After helping Hakim ready the M270, Rodney had taken off from their storage facility 35 minutes ago. Getting to the prison early would have drawn too much attention and blown everything, while arriving late could have meant death for Aldo and Jazlyn. As usual, Rodney was right on schedule.

Finally, Aldo turned to get a good look at the woman he was willing to risk everything for. She hadn't been allowed to shower for a few days in that God forsaken prison, and wore an orange jumpsuit with paper shoes, but he had never seen anything more beautiful. He slid closer to her, pulled his gloves off, and wiped a tear from her cheek. She smiled for the first time in months since this horrible ordeal began. She gently caressed his cheek, and stroked his curly hair. Their bodies grew ever closer, savoring the moment they knew would come. She said nothing, but held onto him tightly until they touched down at the airport minutes later.

Brink bumped fists with Rodney before he and Jazlyn got out and jogged towards the Gulfstream V jet that waited on the runway. Brink left most of his equipment in the chopper, and Jazlyn had slipped on an oversized black jogging suit covering her prison orange. As the steps of the Gulfstream lowered to the tarmac, Hakim Harrison emerged with a big smile. As he passed Brink on the tarmac, he gave his friend a big hug and a sloppy kiss on the cheek. Though there was only one man in the office at this small rural airport who was engrossed in a romance novel, Hakim had disabled the security cameras just to be sure.

"Everything is set. Don't be a stranger," Hakim said.

Brink nodded and watched as Hakim boarded the R66 with his brother. A minute later they lifted off, and were gone.

Brink boarded the plane and secured the door. He gave the Indian pilot and co-pilot the signal to leave and they obliged. They were former Indian Special Forces, and Soham Gupta's personal pilots. He assured Brink they would die before they spoke a word about any flight Soham had ordered them on given all he had done for their families, but Brink slipped them each a manila envelope with one hundred thousand dollars inside, just to put the icing on the cake.

The runway was a little short, but the ace Indian pilots made it work as they took off with tremendous velocity. In a short time, they would be streaking across the Atlantic while the authorities would just be figuring out what the Hell happened at the Wilson Federal Prison complex.

Brink walked back to the main cabin and removed his body armor. He saw the woman he loved curled up on one of the plush chairs, motioning for him to come closer. When he complied, she stood and grabbed him by both arms. It took just seconds for her to spin him around and push him back into the chair.

She let out a primal scream of joy, jumped into his lap, and kissed him like a woman who hadn't been able to touch her fiancé in months.

CHAPTER 19

Flanked by four other agents, Mark Davis felt his pulse quicken as he approached the front door of Aldo Brink's home on the Potomac. The Sun was just coming up, and the neighborhood was mostly still asleep this early in the morning. He felt he was ready to confront Brink, though he had no illusions about whether the man would be home. Davis knew that a professional of the highest caliber like Brink would never just be sitting at home after pulling off what he had last night at the Wilson Federal Prison complex. Davis hoped that in his haste Brink had inadvertently left some evidence behind. Deputy Director Hodges had ordered the mission to retrieve the evidence, if it existed.

Davis had big plans for his future. He wanted to lead the no name unit and have his woman, Gloria Smith, at his side. He had lured Jazlyn Reyes to the Vice President that night while posing as a Secret Service Agent. Though he hadn't planned on doing it that evening, when his lover Gloria identified Reyes as the mark, he went along. He could never say no to her. Deep down he knew she had power over him, but he was so afraid of losing her that he acquiesced to all her demands.

As he entered the house he was surprised at its contemporary and elegant design. He had pictured a hard man like Aldo Brink living in something more modest and dingy. The agents fanned out and checked every room in the house.

"Clear!" each agent said, as they moved through the house.

"Sir, the house is clear," Davis said, as the voice of his boss Sam Hodges came over his earpiece.

"Make a careful inspection. Any detail could be important," Hodges said.

What was once a beautiful home was reduced to a complete mess in short order. The agents rifled the drawers, cut into the furniture, and generally turned over every rock. They came up empty, with one exception.

As soon as Davis entered, he saw Brink's smartphone on the small table next to the couch. Brink no doubt left it behind quite a while ago so Langley couldn't track him by it. As the agents continued to search the house, Davis took to examining Brink's phone. He didn't expect to find anything useful on it, but he had to check it out just to be sure. There was no way Brink left something behind in such an obvious manner unless he wanted them to find it.

What Davis didn't know was that the second he and his team entered the house, the smartphone's motion detector had sent Brink an encrypted alert halfway around the world. After searching through some meaningless office emails on the phone, its loud ring, indicating a call was coming in, startled him. The caller ID simply registered the call as "unknown." Davis answered it and put it on speaker. He made his voice as non-descript as possible, hoping he would be able to garner some information from whoever was trying to contact Brink.

"I don't like uninvited house guests," Brink said, as Davis immediately recognized the voice of the man that he wanted to supplant at the CIA. "Are you listening, Sam?"

"Yes, I'm here," Hodges said. He had been listening to everything through Davis' ear piece.

"I'm only going to say this once, so pay attention," Brink said. "Let it go." The line went dead.

Davis wasn't sure why, but he felt an overwhelming surge of fear come over him. His survival instinct had completely taken over, and before he knew it, he was in a dead run towards the front door. In seconds, he found himself outside running away as if his life depended on it.

The once lovely house exploded behind him with a concussive force that propelled him into the SUV he arrived in. Broken glass, debris, and flaming leaves rained down on him. His ears were ringing and Sam Hodges' screams for a status report were inaudible as he tried to stand. Stumbling as he assessed his injuries, he felt lucky to be alive. He had cuts on his head, and a piece of shrapnel lodged in his thigh, but he was the lucky one.

As he braced himself against the vehicle, he rose to his feet and saw the smoldering remains of Aldo Brink's home. Brink knew they would come and planned to decapitate the no name unit's operational abilities by taking out as many agents as possible. He rigged the house to blow and used the smartphone as the lookout. They were the only ones the powers that be could trust to bring him in without risking more exposure, and now they were dead.

Davis couldn't help but take Brink's warning to heart, and hoped his superiors would do the same. *Let it go.*

CHAPTER 20

President Richard Wilson sat down in the White House situation room just as the video screens flickered to life. Normally the room would have been filled with people, but today it was a more private affair than usual.

After the military officer had initiated the system he was asked to leave, which in itself was not all that unusual. There were many important instances when the President had private discussions with his most trusted aides and cabinet officials. There would be no record of this meeting, as all recording devices were disabled.

The President was joined by his Chief of Staff and by Chris Spencer, the head of his protection detail. On the video monitors were the Director and Deputy Director of the CIA, Donald Abraham and Sam Hodges.

"Mr. President, we can say with absolute certainty that Aldo Brink was the man responsible for the assault on the prison last night. Nine guards were killed, while two were wounded by a combination of firearms and explosives. Jazlyn Reyes escaped with Brink aboard a helicopter. We assume he had at least two accomplices, but we can't be sure. He is the only one on the security tape and I personally identified the yellow skull mask he wore. It was a calling card of his," Hodges explained. "Per your orders, I had an agent destroy the security tapes at the source. He knows nothing of the contents. I personally destroyed the only digital copy, so we are clear to put out any story you desire. The fact is though, he wanted us to know he did it, and he knew you would want the tape destroyed."

"Thank you, Sam. You have done great work under tough circumstances. I appreciate all you've done," Wilson said. "Options?"

Donald Abraham, the keeper of the darkest secrets in Washington spoke next. "Sir, our options are limited if we want to keep the story in play. Brink decapitated our ability to deal with him when he blew up his house this morning with our no name unit agents inside. We only have two left and they are young and inexperienced."

"So, what are you suggesting Don?" President Wilson asked.

"Sir, as difficult as this is to say, I suggest we let it go."

"What?"

"We let it go just like Brink said. We say we are conducting a massive manhunt for her, but in truth we do next to nothing. We leak to the media that her drug associates rescued her and she could be anywhere. This will keep the narrative of Thornburg the statesman in play.

Brink has no charges against him. There is no evidence that he did anything. We can't prosecute him or arrest him. All he wants is to be left alone with her."

"I understand your point, but can we really just let him go? He killed innocent people."

"With all due respect, Mr. President," Abraham said. "So have you and every other man to hold the office when in pursuit of America's national interest. This is not the kind of guy we are going to pick up in some French Internet café through a tip from Interpol. He's too smart. You're damn lucky he didn't come back here and kill all of us for what we've done."

Abraham knew he shouldn't have let it get this far. His mind had started to fail him, but that was no excuse in his line of work. He just wasn't as razor sharp as he used to be. Still, he thought he could stop this before it went any further, and before more people were killed needlessly.

"We still need to take him out," the President said in a matter-of-fact tone.

"He has already taken a chunk out of our operational capability. Say we find him, then what? What if we track him down and take a shot at him and we miss? He will come back here and raise holy Hell. I trust that is the last thing you want right now."

"You're right of course," Wilson said. "Sam, do you agree with Don?"

"Yes sir, I do. As crazy as it sounds, Brink is no threat to anyone right now. But if we move against him, he will be."

The Chief of Staff got the President's attention next. "They go away, and we ride the sympathy of the American people to any domestic initiative we want," he said.

"Then we are all in agreement. Don, Sam, I want you to terminate all efforts to apprehend or otherwise deal with Aldo Brink and Jazlyn Reyes, but conduct a token effort as you suggested to keep up appearances. Feed the FBI whatever you want so they look busy, but make sure all they end up doing is chasing their tails. When we are ready, we will spoon feed them our version. I want them to think that they actually cracked the case! Next, we leak to the press that her escape is the result of a brazen drug cartel."

With that, the video screens flickered off. President Wilson was ready to put this terrible ordeal behind him. Thornburg had put him in a terrible position and it finally blew up in his face, resulting in his death. Now, he could plan the rest of his Presidency and go down in history the way he wanted to. He was no longer a slave to an incompetent Vice President who acted as a human doomsday device to his administration. They were going to pull it off.

They only had to do one thing for it to work. Leave Aldo Brink and his fiancée, alone.

CHAPTER 21

Gloria Smith had just upgraded her hotel suite when Sam Hodges called. She was sick of living in a small cramped room, but failed to mention to her boss that she charged the CIA for it. She thought she deserved better. Hodges had called to tell her the news. She and agent Mark Davis were to terminate all efforts to find Aldo Brink and Jazlyn Reyes. They were also instructed to never discuss the issue again.

They would be rewarded for their work thus far by being given the opportunity to rebuild the no name unit from scratch. Gloria and her lover would be the cornerstones.

Still, she couldn't help but feel unfulfilled. She didn't want to be handed this opportunity, because Brink killed everyone else. She wanted to earn it, but she also wanted the intoxicating feeling that conquering Aldo Brink would bring. At the very least, she wanted to size him up face to face. She needed a shot at him, but her hopes of meeting him had been stolen away.

As she stared across the room at Mark Davis, she felt contempt for him. He had walked straight into a trap set by Aldo Brink and had gotten his entire team killed. Had she been with him, she would have suffered the same fate. Somehow, he had escaped alive by running while the others stayed in the house. Aldo Brink would have stayed and tried to warn everyone. He would have never left his team to die, and if that meant his life would end, so be it. Gloria knew Mark was no Aldo Brink, but the thought of working with him for years to come at the no name unit was something she didn't even want to think about.

Gloria was supremely confident. She acted impulsively with Thornburg, but her instincts had been proven right, she thought. She was told to wait, but it had been a perfect opportunity. She saw Thornburg eyeing Jazlyn Reyes at the party. It was a perfect set up. Still, Gloria wondered how she could have missed Brink. The fact that she was within feet of him at the party tormented her every dream. She wondered how she would have acted had she known the woman was Brink's fiancée. Would she have still gone through with it, or would she have waited and stuck to the original plan?

Gloria wondered what kind of a woman Jazlyn Reyes was. A man like Aldo Brink couldn't possibly be happy with an average woman, she thought. Her egomania began to take over as she inevitably began to think that he would be happier with a woman like herself. She understood his craft and lifestyle, after all. She could support him in every way.

"Mark, my love. We must go after Brink."

"But our orders explicitly say…"

"To Hell with our orders! If we want to forge our own path together, this must not be hanging over our heads. I'm surprised you're so scared of him. The bastard tried to kill you!"

So, it began. Gloria was a master at manipulating men. She zeroed in on their insecurities and used her feminine wiles to her maximum advantage. Mark Davis was nothing more to her than a means to an end. She would kill him herself, but she wanted to extract every ounce of usefulness from him first. She thought, why let an obedient man go to waste? One day she hoped to meet a man who wouldn't be so easily manipulated. Perhaps that was why she wanted to meet Aldo Brink so badly, even at the risk of her own life. He had not seen her, and had no idea she was involved in what happened to Jazlyn. Maybe she could get close to him if the right situation presented itself?

"Why do you speak to me this way?" he asked.

"I'm sorry my love, but I need you to be strong for me. I can't live looking over my shoulder wondering when Brink might be coming up behind me."

"Gloria, he has no reason to come back here. He wants to be left alone with his woman. He can do that now. Why would he risk upsetting that?" he asked.

Of course Mark was right, and Gloria knew it. She had plenty of tricks up her sleeve though. "Mark, you know as much about him as I do. You know he never follows normal procedure. He is unpredictable."

Mark moved towards her. He reached for her shoulder but she pulled away and went to the window. She sighed, refusing to look at him.

"I will protect you," Davis said as he tried to touch her again.

"Please leave. I don't want you here."

That was it. She had him. Mark picked up his jacket and started towards the door. As he walked away, Gloria whimpered by the window just loud enough for him to hear. He stopped, and turned towards her.

"We'll find him together, my love. Once we're done with him, he will never bother us again."

Gloria turned, and approached him. She caressed his cheek and nodded her approval of him just before the kiss. As they embraced, Gloria stroked his body as she whispered into his ear. "Good, because I know how to find him."

CHAPTER 22

Jazlyn stood on the balcony of Soham's estate in Panaji. Not long ago, she faced a life sentence and perhaps even the death penalty, and now she was being treated like royalty by the loyal staff of a billionaire. Besides Soham and his longtime butler Raj, none of the staff had any idea who she was, and that's how it would stay. She looked a bit different now with a new haircut and hair color, and even if one of the staff recognized her they would never betray Soham by speaking about anything that went on inside his home.

She had wracked her brain as to what happened that fateful night. For the life of her she couldn't recall actually stabbing the man. She remembered him flirting with her shamelessly and being quite inappropriate, when she felt a wave of dizziness. Her strength oozed out of her body as she found herself sprawled across the desk with him on top of her. Her arms were flailing wildly as her vision blurred.

She grabbed papers and other items of no consequence but then must have grabbed the letter opener and stabbed him. Her fingerprints were on it after all, and she had bruises on her neck and face.

The fear she felt in prison was gone. They couldn't hurt her anymore. The man she loved made sure of that. She knew her fiancé wasn't a schoolteacher, but seeing him in action was quite a sight to behold. He had killed people to free her while showing no regard for his own life. For a brief moment after her escape, she worried that this would permanently change how she viewed the man she loved, or even if her feelings for him would change. This terrified her more than a death sentence.

The fact remained that she would be in prison for the rest of her life if it hadn't been for Aldo, so who was she to complain about how he achieved the result that she prayed for every night while in that Godforsaken prison? Soon, the answer came to her.

She felt genuine regret with the loss of life, but her freedom overwhelmed it. If that made her a bad person, then so be it. She was not the one who made this necessary. The man who tried to rape her and the people who covered it up were the ones responsible for the people at the prison being killed. If she had been treated fairly, they would be alive today. Jazlyn wondered if these thoughts were just her way of coping with the situation, but as the days passed she kept coming back to one thing. She was free, and didn't care why.

Jazlyn knew of Soham Gupta. He was one of the wealthiest people in the world. His exploits earned international recognition for being a major force behind India's rise from poverty. She had no idea how Aldo knew the titan of industry at all, let alone how he knew him well enough to help him hide his fugitive fiancée. Jazlyn expressed her gratitude to Soham when they arrived in the dead of night, but the billionaire deflected it. After she enjoyed a night's sleep in an actual bed for the first time in months, Soham explained things to her the next morning over breakfast while Aldo spent the morning arranging some longer term housing for them.

Jazlyn wasn't surprised to hear that Aldo had saved Soham's daughter, disobeying his orders in the process. She had seen up close how kind Aldo was, and how he genuinely cared for others many times. Yet, she had also seen him gun down prison guards with shocking precision. Jazlyn was a logical person, and came to the same conclusion Brink did. The bottom line was that this was not their fault. They did not start this, but Aldo would make damn sure that he would finish it by any means necessary.

When Priyanka pulled up a chair for breakfast with them, and told Jazlyn what Aldo had rescued her from, she fully understood why Soham would risk everything he had to help her. While unaware of all the details, Priyanka knew that Aldo had essentially done the same thing for Jazlyn that he did for her.

Priyanka would die before she sold out Aldo Brink. She had experience with torture in the past, and knew she would die before she ever spoke a word about Aldo and Jazlyn. If it was discovered what Soham was doing, everything he worked for would be gone in the blink of an eye. Soham however, assured them both that the risk to him was quite minimal and that they shouldn't worry about such things.

"My dear, the government in this country couldn't touch me even if they had a video of me robbing a bank," he said.

While it sounded grandiose, Soham wasn't far off the mark. He had many friends across the political spectrum and in the halls of power, and he was adored by the people for all his work. There would be riots in the streets if the government started making allegations or in any way moved against Soham Gupta, the protector of India. More importantly, there was no evidence he had done anything to help with Jazlyn's escape.

The plan was to stay here with Soham for a few days, and then move a few miles north to a waterside home that Brink was in the process of renting for them. That would be their medium term housing, but Brink had other long term plans. He did not anticipate the government coming after them, and even if they did they had no idea where he was. The stash in Virginia was not his only one, and if the government didn't let the issue of Jazlyn Reyes drop, he would be back to retrieve another one. They didn't want that.

Still, there was always the issue of someone accidentally stumbling onto them or some other element that was impossible to foresee. Because of this, they would live under new identities that Brink had created months ago for both of them. Jazlyn's beautiful long dark hair had to be cut shorter, and dyed blond.

She worried about what her parents would think about all this. Fortunately, Aldo had discreetly passed word to them that she was fine, and he would be with her. He didn't tell them where they would be, but said that in the future when he was sure they weren't being monitored, they could travel and see their daughter again. This put Jazlyn's mind at ease.

"Aldo thought of everything," she said.

"That's what he does, my dear," Soham said. "Ganesha won't even be able to help them if they don't leave you alone. It is for this reason that they most assuredly will."

CHAPTER 23

Taylor Ross knew he should have seen it coming. Just his luck that the one day he goes home instead of sleeping at Langley, he gets abducted, he thought. Someone had grabbed him from behind as he exited his car at the apartment he rented. He felt an injection, and then after a few seconds, went limp. Now, he was in a chair with his wrists handcuffed behind his back, and a black hood over his head. He wasn't in pain, but did feel a bit nauseous.

The light blinded him when the black hood was abruptly yanked off. Squinting gave him little relief from the burning bright light pointed right at him. When his eyes finally adjusted to the surroundings, he immediately knew his captor. Taylor cursed himself for not recognizing the man when he saw him snooping around outside his office dressed as a janitor.

Mark Davis stood before him, wearing surgical gloves. "What the Hell is this about, man?" Taylor asked.

"Your friend, Aldo Brink."

"I barely know him. I run tech for him just like I run it for you and everyone else in the unit. We've been ordered to let this issue drop. Didn't you get the memo?"

"We missed it," said Gloria Smith as she exited the shadows.

"Oh good, finally I get to talk to the man in charge," Taylor said.

Gloria slapped him across the face. Taylor knew all about Gloria and Mark's "relationship." He also knew how Gloria manipulated her men into doing what she wanted. He saw it all in her file during her recruiting process. Hodges thought it would be a plus to have a female agent in the unit that could infiltrate areas that a man couldn't.

"Where is Brink?" Mark asked.

"Who?"

Mark picked up a heavy steel chain and whipped it across Taylor's chest. He cried out in pain.

"Are you insane? Brink is a professional. He would never tell me where he was going! He would know I might be put in a situation just like this and wouldn't want me to have the information to give up, you dumb whipped son of a bitch!"

Mark and Gloria knew he had a point. Brink would never leave such information with someone as flimsy as Taylor Ross. "Someone with resources must have helped him somehow. Who would owe him a favor?" Mark asked.

"What is your plan? What do you hope to accomplish by finding him? It's over. He's gone. Move on with your life. Oh my God, did she put you up to this? Is that it?"

This time Gloria punched him with her brass knuckles causing Taylor to spit some blood onto the floor. "My lover can handle Aldo Brink. He's not afraid of him. He's a real man who makes his own decisions."

"Yeah, OK," Taylor said as he fought back laughter. "Do you two fools know what he's going to do to you if you go after him? He's going to come back here and kill you." Taylor turned to Mark. "He is going to kill your psycho bitch girlfriend right in front of you, and then he's going to kill you. Is that what you want?"

"That's not going to happen."

"This bitch is going to get you killed! Wake up, dumbass!"

Mark Davis moved off into the darkness. He returned a moment later with a suitcase. After giving Taylor a wink, he placed it on a nearby table. When he opened it, Taylor saw the various instruments inside, and wasn't eager to come in contact with them.

"The chain should be enough, but if not, there are always these."

"I don't know where he is."

"I believe you. But you also know all about his past operations, or at least most of them. You know the things that even the bosses don't. You might know who owes him a favor. You just need your memory jogged."

After he coughed up his secrets, they would leave him chained and gagged. Mark wanted to kill the little punk, but Gloria talked him into letting him live in case they needed to question him later. The plan went to Hell though when Mark worked Taylor over a bit too hard. Taylor was going to die if they left him there, so if he was to survive, dumping him at the hospital became their only option.

The authorities at the hospital would ask Taylor a lot of questions, and this was a risk, but ultimately it didn't matter. They were going to disappear, and there existed a good chance that Taylor wouldn't talk to the police or hospital authorities anyway. He would wait until he could talk to Brink and wouldn't discuss company dirty laundry with local law enforcement.

Gloria looked on and smiled. She felt a jolt of ecstasy as Mark whipped Taylor with the chain, over and over again.

CHAPTER 24

Jazlyn knew there was no going back now. She missed her old life terribly, but given the alternative she was thrilled to be standing on the rear deck of the waterfront home Aldo had leased for them ten miles north of Soham's estate. Rustic and colorful, the house had two levels, and wasn't visible from the main road nearest it.

Entering the house, she found Aldo waiting for her in the kitchen. On the table were fresh scrambled eggs, potatoes, and toast her fiancé had prepared just for her.

"Sit down, Jaz. Have some breakfast. I know it's been a whirlwind and you haven't been eating much."

Jazlyn nodded in agreement. This morning was the first time she felt normal, as if she was a tourist on an exotic vacation rather than an international fugitive. Aldo poured her a glass of orange juice and sat down with her. "Eat up," Aldo said with a smile.

"I'll never forget what you did for me. I need you to know that."

"You already told me. I know. You don't have to keep thanking me. Well, you can thank me by eating your breakfast before it gets cold. You need to replenish your strength after everything that's happened."

Jazlyn ate everything on her plate.

Later that day Aldo, Jazlyn, and Priyanka went shopping. One of the things Brink did while planning her escape was to take a variety of clothes and personal items from Jazlyn's condo that he knew she would want for an extended "vacation." They were waiting for her in Soham's jet, on the night of the escape. Still, she needed more clothes, especially if she wanted to blend in. Priyanka seemed to know every clothing store in the country, and had a wonderful time helping Jazlyn out. Priyanka was an only child and always thought it would be wonderful to have a sister. She forged a bond with Jazlyn immediately. Aldo Brink had saved them both, a fact that was not lost on either woman.

Priyanka led Jazlyn to all the finest boutiques, and arranged private access to the shops to avoid any crowds or curious people that might look into who Priyanka was out shopping with. Aldo loved watching them find outfits and then come out from the changing room to model for him. Jazlyn was having fun again, something she hadn't done in a long time and Brink wanted it to continue. When Priyanka picked out a beautiful Sari for Jazlyn to wear, Brink's smile was ear to ear.

"Aldo, look how pretty she is in it. She must have some Indian in her," Priyanka said as they watched her emerge from the changing room. The Sari, a popular garment in the region, looked lovely on her. Its brilliant red color looked exotic with her newly dyed blond hair.

"Priyanka, next time I need to dress you up Brazilian style."

"Ooh, that sounds fun!"

Brink did his best to get Jazlyn back into the swing of the real world. Obviously, living in India was a big change from her condo back in Washington, but she had already begun to adjust. They had plenty of money and could live off interest payments and dividends easily, so getting by on a daily basis posed no problem. Though India boasted a large English speaking population, Jazlyn resolved to learn the native language. Each night, she would lie in bed with Aldo and they would read from a how-to book Soham had suggested. They practiced with each other like a normal couple would while on vacation.

They were lying in bed when Brink noticed Jazlyn seemed a little down. "Are you OK?" he asked.

"Do you still want to marry me? I don't blame you if you don't," she said. Brink tossed the book aside and grabbed her hand.

"Of course, I do. What kind of a question is that?"

"If you stay with me, you can never go home, because I can never go home."

"Let me worry about that. Ya never know what can happen in the future. I don't care where we live or what name is on your driver's license. You are still the woman I fell in love with."

"I just hate that I put you in this situation."

"Hey, you didn't put me in this situation. Those bastards who decided it was OK for you to suffer are the ones that put us where we are. If you will still have me, I'm not going anywhere. You think I would do all that back at the prison for anyone?"

She got it. "No."

"I did that at the prison for you because I love you, but I also did it for me. I had selfish reasons. I couldn't live with knowing you were there. I can't live without you."

She slid closer to him, hugged him, and kissed him. "I love you."

"Don't worry. Everything is going to be fine."

"OK"

"I want to marry you. I thought once things cool down, we could meet your parents somewhere and have an intimate wedding so they can see their little girl on her big day."

"You really do think of everything, don't you?"

"Yes, I do."

CHAPTER 25

Mark Davis looked at the dusty brick buildings of Karachi, Pakistan. He had discovered a lead on Aldo Brink and while it wasn't a sure thing, process of elimination told him it was a good place to start.

Taylor Ross was loyal to Brink far more than he gave him credit for. He inflicted severe pain on the young man, but he still hadn't broken. Mark augmented the torture with mind altering drugs.

Once they started to kick in, Taylor let something slip about Brink's past. On a mission in Europe Brink disobeyed orders and saved a young woman, rather than track down the target he was assigned to eliminate. Brink put a bullet in the man's head a year later, but that mattered little now.

That was all that Taylor knew. He had no idea who the girl was and how this could fit into finding Brink today. His lover, Gloria Smith suggested they do a search for wealthy or otherwise important individuals reporting their daughters missing around that time. Sure enough, they found Indian billionaire Soham Gupta, who had reported his daughter missing. She was last seen in Prague, the same country Brink had been in. Gloria made the connection. Perhaps the man owed Brink and would do anything to repay such a debt? It was a long shot, but since they had no other theories, Mark and Gloria decided it was at least worth looking into.

Gloria traveled ahead to India. She saw a blond haired Jazlyn walk the local market with Priyanka Gupta. She couldn't believe her luck. She followed them, but was too afraid of running into Aldo Brink so she pulled away at the last moment. She did however see the road where they turned. After chatting up a local real estate agent, it was clear where they were hiding. She returned later that night to get a closer look, where she eyed the rented villa.

She knew she needed to move fast. Brink wouldn't stay in one place for too long this early after the prison raid. Once he left India, there would be no way to track him barring some miraculous stroke of luck. They couldn't wait. They had to move on him, now.

When she told Mark this news, he wanted to call for backup through official channels in a futile effort to convince their bosses that they could eliminate Brink without any blowback, but Gloria convinced him not to. After all, they were not even supposed to be doing this. They were under strict orders to leave the issue alone for a host of reasons. Gloria wanted Mark to go in alone. To her chagrin, he smartly refused, and travelled to Pakistan to get help.

When he reached the meeting point, he checked the safety on his pistol. He didn't expect trouble, but in this part of the world, things could go to Hell quickly. The Pakistani mercenaries he would hire hated America and better yet, they hated Aldo Brink, even though they didn't know it.

For years, Brink had been a thorn in the side of the terror cells inside Pakistan. He would attack in the dead of night with a small team, while wearing a yellow skull mask. The terror groups came to know him as "The Skull." The Skull had done tremendous damage to their cause, so much so that they had pulled back from their Afghanistan operations where they were dedicated to kicking out the Americans.

When the four men arrived, Mark thought they looked sufficiently nasty. He asked if they wanted a shot at killing The Skull and his woman. They jumped at the chance and left with Davis. The five of them were on a plane headed to India a few hours later.

Back home, Gloria thought of Aldo Brink ripping her lover apart along with his team of mercenaries. These men were walking into a death trap and they didn't even know it. After Brink had killed her lover and his team, she would be in position to cozy up to him.

The thought of being with him sent shivers down her spine. Finally, she had found someone who could tame her. If everything went according to plan, she would have Aldo Brink's trust.

CHAPTER 26

As Mark Davis ran through the narrow streets of Panaji, he wondered where it all went wrong. How could this be happening? They outnumbered him five to one, but somehow he knew they were coming. Had he spotted them earlier somehow? Mark had no idea, but he couldn't worry about that now. Getting away was all that mattered. Being pursued by Aldo Brink terrified him enough, but the thought of being caught by him shook his very soul.

The streets were filled with compact cars and auto rickshaws. The narrow side streets meant less of a chance of being hit by the countless vehicles on the main roads, but it gave him little room to maneuver if Brink caught up with him. Mark didn't know the streets well and eventually the maze of downtown Panaji only gave him one option. When he reached Mahatma Gandhi Road he turned right. The pedestrian traffic wasn't high enough to blend into so he turned left immediately and headed north. His only chance was the ferry, if he could make it in time.

Mark still couldn't understand what happened. The Sun was just coming up when they first attacked the house. Mark Davis and his four hired guns crept through the grass, illuminated only by faint rays of sunlight. The house came into view. They saw no movement and no lights inside. When they reached the porch, the floorboards creaked and the team of assassins froze, hoping the killer of killers hadn't heard their blunder. When nothing happened, they assumed the best and entered through the front door which to their surprise was unlocked.

They ascended the steps quietly and confidently, but when they reached the bedroom door the weight of the moment caught up with them. Aldo Brink was on the other side of that door. They had the drop on him, but what if they missed? Sensing the indecision among his comrades, Mark masked his fear by counting down from three with his hand. The Pakistanis nodded and raised their pistols. Mark barged into the bedroom.

The men emptied their magazines into the bed. The second they started to reload, three quick flashes of light came from the hallway. Mark looked to his left and saw three of his hired guns lying on the floor, each with a gunshot wound to the head.

"He's in the hallway!"

The remaining Pakistani, perhaps out of a sense of honor raced to the hallway. His choice proved a poor one as Mark saw another flash of light followed immediately by a loud boom as the last of his assassins fell.

Brink stepped out of the darkened hallway. Mark froze. He knew if he attempted to reload his pistol, Brink would kill him straight away, so he did the only thing he could. He ran.

Mark dropped his gun, turned, and jumped head first out the second floor window. Rolling across the overhang, he grabbed the gutter and swung his legs over the side, dropping safely to the ground below. When he reached his car, he found all four tires flat. Brink had slashed them and followed the band of assassins as they moved into the house. Davis felt like a fool. He thought he could out maneuver Aldo Brink. His arrogance had exploded in his face and turned the hunter into the hunted.

He huffed and puffed as he ran to the main road where his luck improved. An auto rickshaw was on its way down the road. Mark jumped into the street and waved his arms at the man driving. When he stopped, Mark tried to throw him out, but the man put up quite a struggle which gave Brink a chance to catch up. Just as Mark got control of the vehicle and hit the accelerator, Brink jumped into the backseat and hit his would-be assassin in the side of the head with a vicious elbow strike.

Brink recognized the man immediately. He was new to the no name unit and apparently had survived the explosion at his house on the Potomac. The arrogance of those bastards in Washington, Brink thought. They would send this amateur to try and take him down? Were their egos so badly bruised that they were willing to resort to this? Brink knew he would make them pay for their continued belligerence.

The auto rickshaw sped towards the urban area of Panaji. The morning commute was just getting underway as people in India got to work very early. Mark fought for control, but could only swerve wildly as he tried to block Brink's elbow strikes. Traffic backed up quickly, so Mark tried to slow down in time, but was too late. He jerked the wheel and slammed the auto rickshaw into a shop on the corner. The shop's front window shattered as the auto rickshaw barreled through it. Mark bailed out of the vehicle. As he started to run, the broken glass that covered him fell to the ground.

His bloody face grimaced as he took off down the crowded street. He had to lose Brink, but how? Turning at this first opportunity, he went down a narrow thoroughfare and cut through a local butcher shop. As he stumbled through the shop, Mark considered grabbing a knife from the counter. No, his best bet was still the ferry, he thought.

As he sprinted towards salvation, the water came into view. The last of the passengers were boarding the small ferry. As the attendant signaled for the captain to get underway, Mark pushed himself harder. His lungs were burning with the hot, dusty air. His morbid fear of being caught overcame his exhaustion as he raced for the ferry just as it pulled away from the pier.

He didn't think he would make it, but he jumped anyway. His legs were submerged as he clung to the rear of the boat. The passengers screamed at him in Hindi. He had no idea what they were saying, but he assumed it wasn't complimentary. To his relief, they helped him up regardless. He quickly handed some money to the attendant before any monetary dispute could arise. Mark tried to catch his breath as he looked back at the pier.

Aldo Brink stood tall and smiling. He pointed at Mark for a moment with one finger, and then gestured quickly toward his own eye with the same one. Brink would be seeing him again. The ferry pulling further away did little to ease Mark's discomfort. He had committed an error that meant inevitable death.

Brink walked away, blood boiling. He'd gotten word from Soham's security people that some outsiders were poking around town, but he would have spotted them anyway. Pakistan and India weren't exactly on the best of terms and four Pakistanis walking around downtown Panaji with a white American who were asking lots of questions stuck out like a sore thumb.

He gathered up her things and had Jazlyn stay with Soham who had enough security to occupy Paris, while he trailed Mark Davis and his team. He hoped they would lead him to someone important, but he wasn't that lucky.

Later that night, he disposed of the bodies in the house, cleaned the place up, and decided that would be the last night for him and Jazlyn's rustic vacation home. The lease ran for six months, but now that its location was blown, it served no useful purpose. He wanted to stay there longer until the media attention from the prison break died down, but that wasn't possible now. Aldo Brink wanted to be a gentleman. "Let it go," he told them, but they didn't listen.

If this is how they wanted it, then that was fine with him. He would end it with unrelenting violence, and he would bring it to their doorstep.

Brink pulled a small envelope from his pocket. A local boy hand-delivered it to him and said a woman paid him five thousand Rupees to do so. Pulling the letter out of the envelope, he read it again and chuckled. Someone had tried to warn him about the attack. The point was moot as Brink sniffed it out early, but who would warn him and why?

The paper had a phone number on one side and a short message on the other.

Mark Davis framed her. He's out of control.
He's coming to kill you. Please help. Gloria Smith.

CHAPTER 27

Gloria Smith had all her bases covered. If by some miracle her lover killed Aldo Brink, then she wouldn't have to worry about him ever finding out about her. If Brink killed him, then she would be on his good side since she warned him. Given Brink's skill level, she knew he would spot the assassination team, but her letter of warning made it appear her concern was genuine.

Gloria felt quite pleased with herself. She had everyone on a string, and no one suspected a thing. Even the man who shared a bed with her remained oblivious. She sent her clueless lover into a death trap. The power felt intoxicating to her. As a young girl, she felt trapped and weak, but now she held all the keys, and pulled all the strings.

When Mark Davis returned to Gloria's DC hotel suite no worse for wear, save for a few cuts and bruises, she thought fast.

"My love, what happened?" she asked.

Davis explained what happened in India. "I think he recognized me."

"He what!?"

"I could tell he knew who I was. I've been in the unit a bit longer than you, so he probably knows about me. You are brand new so he's not aware of you, yet."

This worked out quite well, Gloria thought. Brink would no doubt be coming back home to kill Mark and anyone else involved, and given that she warned him once already, she would be in position to assist him. It would be a dangerous high wire act, but that's what made her life worth living. "We will wait until the right moment, and then we will bring him down. Brink doesn't know about me, so that will give us an advantage," she said.

Someone as weak and gullible as Mark Davis didn't deserve to be alive, she thought. More importantly, he didn't deserve to be with her.

"We must lay low and get ready. Brink will be coming," Mark said.

"We'll be ready for him."

Gloria had never been this far on the edge before, but that's what made it enjoyable.

CHAPTER 28

Donald Abraham entered the backseat of his Cadillac Escalade ESV, exhausted from a long day's work. He exhaled as the security officer slammed the heavy armored door shut and signaled to the driver to get going. As it pulled away from the CIA headquarters security gate, he stretched his tired legs, leaned his head back, and closed his eyes. He would be retired soon, certainly by the end of this administration, if not sooner. Keeping decades of secrets took its toll on the human spirit. If most Presidents notoriously aged twice as fast as a normal person due to the stress of the job, a CIA director must age three times as fast, Abraham thought.

It would take about twenty-five minutes to arrive at his townhouse, and Abraham looked forward to relaxing in his library in a comfortable leather chair. A glass of bourbon would complete the night. He would watch a little TV and then retire for the evening. Living as a widower made him quite lonely, and he thought of his late wife often. He would be with her again soon, he thought.

Maybe his fatigue had something to do with it, but he hadn't realized the driver missed the turn. Once he realized, Abraham didn't have to say a thing. He knew his situation, and he knew he wasn't in control of it anymore.

The Escalade pulled off to the side of the road and ducked into an alley. The driver turned around.

Though Aldo Brink looked angry, Donald Abraham wasn't scared of him. At his age, Abraham wasn't concerned with death. He trained himself over the years to never worry about something he couldn't control. Doing so would inevitably cripple your decision making in the future. "Is my security detail dead?" he asked.

"Maybe."

"Damn it Aldo, they had nothing to do with this! They are innocent."

"Relax, they are still breathing, but that can change."

"They have nothing to do with this!"

"Since when do you care about innocent people?"

The keeper of secrets and lies slumped back in his seat. "My job is to protect the United States of America, not your girlfriend. I am sorry what happened to her, but..."

Brink drew his HK45 pistol and aimed it at his boss. "I don't think you want to go there."

"If you wanted me dead, I would be, so what is this about?"

"It's about Mark Davis and four Pakistanis who came to kill me," Brink said.

"I don't know anything about that. I was in the Oval Office when the President gave the order to fake a manhunt and to let you and Jazlyn go."

"I suppose you don't know anything about Taylor Ross being tortured by Mark Davis to try and learn about my past with the company?"

"You'd be correct. This is the first I'm hearing of it. I certainly didn't order him to do that. We have not been able to contact Mark Davis, or Gloria Smith. They are in the wind."

"I know you didn't order it, and that's why you're still alive," Brink said. "Taylor gave me a call. He was recovering in the hospital, but I had two friends pick him up. They are going to look after him to make sure he can heal in peace without fear of any more visits from your agents."

"Is he OK?"

"He will be."

"Good, I'm glad to hear it."

Brink smiled. "So tell me about Mark Davis."

"He's new. Hodges brought him in and gave him some small assignments. After you killed the field agent roster with that bomb at your house, he was only one of two left. Gloria Smith is the other one, but she is new and I don't know much about her. Hodges would though."

"What else?"

"Sam Hodges can be an asshole, but he isn't stupid. He would never send that amateur to attack you and he certainly wouldn't sign off on using Pakistanis to help.

Whoever sent them after you, is someone who has an ulterior motive."

"And what could that be?"

"Only Mark Davis would know, and since Hodges brought him in, maybe he has some idea." Abraham leaned forward. "How far are you willing to take this?"

"Further than you can possibly imagine, but that's up to you and the rest of the power brokers." Brink holstered his pistol. "The keys are in the ignition. If I were you, I'd get out of here before the local gang bangers see a nice ride where it doesn't belong."

Brink got out of the car and walked down the alley, disappearing into the night. Abraham drove away a minute later. Deep down, he couldn't help but feel ashamed. Maybe earlier in his career he could have stopped this from getting out of control, but not now. He felt ashamed that he didn't try harder to put a stop to this. Jazlyn Reyes should have never been imprisoned. That was all water under the bridge at this point. Nothing could be done anymore.

Abraham knew not to worry about things he couldn't control, and Aldo Brink fell squarely into that category.

CHAPTER 29

Brink sat in the living room of Sam Hodges' upscale townhouse. The Deputy Director of the CIA would be home any minute, and he didn't mind waiting. Answers were in short supply and he wanted to know the whole story, or at the very least everything that Hodges knew. Darkness filled the room except for the faint moonlight streaking in through the bay window.

Jingling keys broke the silence. Sam Hodges entered and locked the door behind him. He walked through the living room where Brink startled him.

"Have a seat, Sam."

"Aldo," Hodges said. He walked slowly with his hands visible to Brink and sat down in the chair across from him.

"I know you have security outside. If you call them, yell for them, or signal for them in any way, I'm going to have to use this," Brink said as he showed his gun to Hodges. "And if I use this, then I'm going all the way. Get it?"

"Yes."

"So let's talk."

"Why are you back here? I figured you and Jazlyn would be long gone forever."

"Well, that's the thing. We were, but then Mark Davis and a team of Pakistani guns for hire tried to kill us."

"Oh?"

"And someone must have ordered them to do it."

"Did you talk to the old man?" Hodges asked.

"He said I should talk to you. Funny, how you guys have that worked out."

"It's habit. You know that."

"I suppose I do," Brink said.

Brink pulled his pistol from his holster and quickly screwed in a thick black suppressor onto the end of the barrel. The Deputy Director of the CIA squirmed in his seat. "Just ask me what you want to know, Aldo," he said.

"Tell me about Mark Davis."

"He's a young, up and coming operator. He follows orders. I was going to reconstitute the unit with him and the woman he works with. Though, I'm not too sure about her."

"What woman?"

"Gloria Smith."

"I received a note signed Gloria Smith warning me about the attack. It also said something very interesting."

"And what was that?" Hodges asked.

"The note said Mark Davis framed her. I can only assume she referred to Jazlyn. Now tell me, what do you know about that?"

Brink cocked the hammer on his HK45. It was very dark, but Hodges could see the long suppressed barrel pointed at him. "Leave nothing out," Brink said.

"First of all, I didn't order him to attack you. The White House wanted the issue dropped as I'm sure you anticipated. To use your words, we were going to let it go. Now, in terms of Jazlyn being framed, that's a complicated matter."

"Try me," Brink said, still pointing his pistol at Hodges. "You know with these subsonic rounds combined with this suppressor, the only sound will be the click of the slide."

"The President was being blackmailed over Thornburg, so he had to be removed from the equation. You know Thornburg had mistresses. Well, at least three that we know of were pros who worked for a Russian Mafia group. This group is headed by Anton Volodin. You heard of him?"

"Of course, he is former GRU, but still works with them. He has GRU operatives who work for him and they have a quasi-partnership with the Russian intelligence services."

The Russian equivalent to the American CIA was GRU. Created out of the KGB when it disbanded, it routinely engaged in blackmail of foreign government officials. They constantly unearthed dirt on important people and used it to their advantage. Along with assassinations and all manner of espionage, GRU held its own among the most ruthless of international intelligence services.

"Keep going," Brink said.

"Volodin's girls got to talking, and he found out that he had this dirt on the Vice President. He passes it up the chain to GRU in Russia and they threatened to blackmail the President. They want oil contracts, all kinds of concessions on various issues of dispute, on and on."

"So?"

"I was ordered to use Mark Davis and Gloria Smith to kill the Vice President and make it look a certain way. With him gone, the Russians had no leverage. They had pictures and everything. They still could have released them, but it would have been overwhelmed with the grief of the nation, and the White House would have written them off as cheap forgeries designed to discredit the memory of a noble public servant who isn't alive to defend himself. Plus, they knew the VP was a time bomb that could blow up in their faces at any time. He had to be dealt with sooner or later."

"And you just followed this order without question? Killing your own Vice President?"

"Aldo, we've killed people who can do far less damage to the country. You should know that. When the White House gives me an order, I follow it."

"And you wanted to get in good with them so you could get your promotion. Am I getting warm, Sam?"

Hodges smiled. "I just followed my orders from the White House."

"Who at the White House?"

"Who do you think? Starts at the top and goes on down. They are all in it together. Decisions like this aren't made by just one person, but it starts and ends at the top. He had the final decision. Aldo you have to understand, I had no idea Jazlyn was the mark."

"Oh, you had no idea?"

"The operation was supposed to happen a week later, but that dumb bitch Gloria said she saw an opportunity and took it. She didn't even know it was your fiancée. It could have been any woman. She drugged the drinks of the Vice President and Jazlyn. When they passed out, Gloria stabbed Thornburg with the letter opener and then put it in Jazlyn's hands. She put Thornburg's hands around Jazlyn's neck while she was still hazy. That's why she doesn't remember stabbing him, but remembers being choked. A few frames of the security tape were removed so no one ever saw Gloria go into the room. Taylor would have spotted it eventually had Davis not put him out of commission. Mark Davis killed the original pathologist in a staged mugging. We had everything wired from top to bottom."

"Why not just have the VP killed with a bombing or something, and blame it on a terrorist group?" Brink asked.

"We thought about that, but then the rank and file FBI, CIA, and Secret Service would have to be involved more than they already would be. Keeping the story buttoned up would be complicated enough as it is. There is too much info out there on terror cells, and too many inside our own agencies would have questioned the story when nothing indicated an attack was imminent. This way we had one villain, a lone home grown assassin that the intelligence agencies could easily miss, and unfortunately it turned out to be your fiancée, thanks to Gloria."

"You bastards."

"Listen to me. Gloria controls Mark Davis' every move. She is a sociopath who manipulates people. My guess is Gloria had Davis attack you. In her twisted mind, she has a thing for you, wants to be your partner in crime or something."

"Don't worry about them. I have some special plans for them both. Don didn't know about this, did he?"

"No. He could have asked more questions, but no, he didn't know about it. He just tried to cover it up after the fact. Listen, Jazlyn Reyes didn't kill anyone, not in cold blood, and not in self-defense."

Brink stood up and walked closer to the man who would feel all his rage. "And yet, you were going to let her rot in prison for life, or even get the death penalty?"

"It's just business, Aldo," Hodges said.

"For me, it was personal; very personal, you son of a bitch."

The tension in the living room and the ongoing interrogation didn't last. An eruption of gunfire outside meant Aldo Brink would have to deal with something else first.

CHAPTER 30

Hodges hit the floor while Brink darted to the window. One of Hodges' security men crawled for his life across the asphalt of the street. A hefty assassin ended his futile attempt with a shotgun blast to the back.

A solitary street light maintained a vigil over the dark street, as Brink's eyes scanned the kill zone and saw the rest of the security detail, dead. Three armed men were coming up the stairs to the front door as he heard the sound of breaking glass coming from the rear of the house.

"Who might this be, Sam?" Brink asked.

"We are CIA. We have many admirers!"

Brink grabbed Hodges by the back of the neck, and pulled him to his feet. He pushed him into a closet in the kitchen and closed the door, just as two large men entered through the back door after breaking the glass. Brink knew Hodges equipped his home with a security system, but the fact that alarm bells weren't ringing meant it must have been disabled. He moved out of view and into the hallway, ready to strike.

Brink heard something in Russian from one of the men as he walked to a perpendicular position to the hallway. The thud of the big Russian hitting the floor made more noise than the subsonic suppressed hollow point round Brink fired a second earlier. Retreating down the hallway and around the corner, Brink waited by the back stairs. He stomped his feet in place giving the impression that he had sped upstairs to escape the intruders. The next Russian went to a knee and found his comrade with a bullet to the head. Out for blood, he moved decisively down the hallway.

Speed carried critical importance in Brink's line of work, but he learned a long time ago that speed without precision was simply wasted energy waiting to be exploited by your opponent. The Russian hadn't learned this lesson. He came around the corner more worried about getting up the back stairs than about who was waiting for him around the bend. By the time the Russian's eyes saw Brink, his pistol was too far in front of his body for a quick shot.

Brink squeezed the trigger twice, and sent two rounds into the belly of the Russian who tried in vain to position for a shot. The man fell forward to his knees and Brink shot him a final time in the right temple. The Russian went limp, falling face first to the floor, while Brink quietly ascended the steps.

Another Russian stood rifling the drawers in what appeared to be the second floor master bedroom. Knowing he had six rounds left in his ten round magazine, Brink preferred to conserve ammo rather than run the risk of having to reload in the middle of a gunfight. When the Russian turned his back and moved towards the bedroom closet, Brink abandoned his stealth approach and broke into a full sprint. In a few steps, he was at maximum velocity and drop kicked the man with both legs extended, ejecting the Russian assassin out the bedroom window. Brink quickly followed him out the window while protecting his eyes from the broken glass shards. After shimmying down the drain pipe to the grass below, Brink saw the result of his handiwork. The Russian lay dead, having been impaled on the iron garden fence.

He knew he needed to get back inside quickly. They would find Sam Hodges hiding in the closet any minute and Brink needed him alive, for now. Brink waited a moment in the shadows when he saw the remaining two Russians look out the bedroom window at their impaled comrade. They yelled something in their native tongue and went back into the house.

Brink reversed course and climbed back up the drain pipe and into the house. From the top of the front stairs, he could tell the men were moving to the living room, and heading towards the kitchen where Hodges hid in the closet. When one man got a step out of view from the other, Brink slid head first down the railing of the stairs and aimed his pistol at the trailing Russian. After a light squeeze of the trigger, the hollow point entered the back of the man's skull.

The last Russian heard nothing. He had opened the closet door to find a surprisingly calm Sam Hodges. The Russian smiled a toothy grin and held his pistol to the Deputy Director's forehead.

"Anton Volodin sends his regards," the Russian said.

Hodges closed his eyes, and took a breath, only to reopen them when he heard a horrifying scream. As the Russian staggered around trying to regain his balance, Aldo Brink stood next to him, holding a bloody butcher knife. Hodges' eyes scanned left and realized why the Russian had screamed. His pistol had fallen to the ground with his hand still gripping it. Brink had chopped his hand clean off at the wrist with a cooking knife from Hodges' kitchen. While he could have just shot him, Hodges realized Brink wanted the man alive, at least for a short while.

Blood poured from the Russian's stump as he staggered to a chair at the kitchen table. "Do you want me to stop the bleeding?" Brink asked.

"GRU doesn't need help from an American dog!"

"Fine by me," Brink said as he started to walk away.

"Wait! Yes, stop it now! Stop it!"

Brink yanked the Russian out of his chair and pulled him to the stove top. He turned the gas burner on and put the gaping wound into the fire. The Russian squirmed and cried out in terror before passing out from shock.

Hodges took several steps back and covered his nose as the stench of burning flesh filled the air. After the wound's bleeding stopped, Brink motioned for Hodges to come closer. Brink moved the Russian to the counter while he fished a piece of paper from his pocket and handed it to his former boss.

"That's a number to my phone. I want everything you've got on Mark Davis and Gloria Smith sent to my phone so I can download it in one hour! Don't even think about tracing it, because I am going to dump it as soon as I get the files and download them. If after an hour, I don't have the files, or I feel you're trying to play me, I'm going to come back here and cut off more than a hand."

Brink slung the unconscious Russian over his shoulder and headed for the back door. "What about him?" Hodges asked.

"He's coming with me."

CHAPTER 31

The knock on the door didn't startle her. After a long night's sleep, Jazlyn Reyes had been up for half an hour already. It was her best night's sleep in months, but she still felt tired. After putting her robe on, she answered the door.

"Good morning Ms. Reyes." Raj, Soham's longtime butler and confidante greeted her. He held a tray with a croissant and a glass of fresh orange Juice.

"You treat me too well here."

"Any friend of Mr. Brink's is welcome here. A true friend is a rare thing today, so we must take care of them. Don't you agree?"

"Yes, I do. Thank you." Jazlyn took the croissant and juice.

At a lanky 6'6, Raj stood out in a crowd. With the exception of formal parties and events, he rarely wore a suit, but always dressed impeccably. "Mr. Gupta is taking care of some business this morning, so you are stuck with me, I'm afraid."

Jazlyn took a bite from her croissant. "Right, stuck in a palace with a man who waits on me hand and foot. Most people dream of being stuck like that."

"When you're ready, please join me on the terrace near the kitchen. I will prepare you a full breakfast."

"I thought this was breakfast," Jazlyn said as she held up her juice glass and croissant.

"Ganesha should strike me down if I treated an honored guest so poorly."

After a quick shower, Jazlyn dressed and went to the terrace where Raj just finished setting the table. A two burner propane stove had been wheeled out to the terrace along with fresh ingredients. Jazlyn took a seat and watched the Indian butler work his magic.

"I didn't want to leave you here alone while I prepared the food in the kitchen so I thought this would be nice. We can talk while I make it."

"That sounds lovely, Raj."

At first she couldn't believe Aldo knew a billionaire like Soham Gupta whom she'd read about in the newspapers. He not only knew him, but the man felt he owed her fiancé to the point where he willingly assisted in a prison break. Yet, here she sat being treated like royalty.

When Priyanka explained what Aldo did for her, things made a bit more sense. Soham appreciated Aldo's actions and his daughter was worth any price. Aldo had refused any compensation until now, when he needed it to save her.

"I have some inside information that you enjoy eggs, so I will be making you a special Raj omelet, Poori Bhaji, and fresh fruit. The mangos are from this very property."

Jazlyn watched as Raj started to cook from his prepared ingredients. "With all you do here, do you get to see your family often?" Jazlyn asked.

"My mother died when I was young, and I lost the rest of my family during the fighting in Kashmir. Soham and Priyanka are my only family now."

"I'm so sorry. I shouldn't have brought it up."

"Not at all, I enjoy talking about them. I have wonderful memories, even of my mother from when I was a child." Raj sliced some fruit while watching his omelet like a hawk.

"I asked, because I miss mine terribly. I wouldn't let them see me in prison and I feel awful about it. It was so selfish of me. I want to see them again, but I guess I can't. They are older now. What if they pass on before I can see them again?"

"You will see them again, but from what Mr. Brink has said, it is just too dangerous right now. He knows what he's talking about, believe me."

"I know he does," Jazlyn said. "I just have to see them."

"In time, I'm sure you will." Raj folded the omelet with the dexterity of a surgeon. He timed it perfectly so the Poori Bhaji was ready at the same time as the omelet. "Breakfast is served," Raj said as he set the plates down in front of her.

"It looks amazing." Jazlyn took a bite. "Oh wow this is good. I could get used to this. Thank you so much."

"It is my pleasure, Ms. Reyes."

"Aren't you hungry?"

"Don't worry about me. I ate before anyone else in the house got up. I always get an early start to things."

Jazlyn couldn't stop worrying about Aldo. He said she needed to stay with Soham for a while until he took care of a few things. When she asked him what he meant by that, he said she didn't need to worry. He'd risked so much for her already, and she couldn't bear the thought of losing him now, not after all this.

"Do you know where Aldo is and when he's coming back?" Jazlyn asked.

Raj took a seat at the table across from her after refilling her glass of orange juice. "Any smart man would not want to be away from a beautiful woman like you for very long, so I'm sure he will return soon. Mr. Brink is a very smart man."

"So, do you know where he is?"

"He said he needed to take care of some business to make sure you're safe."

"Oh my God. He's in danger all because of me! I still can't believe all this is happening."

Jazlyn didn't want to cry in front of Raj. Her father wasn't in the best of health. He worked so hard for so long to put his little girl through college and now he might never see his daughter again, in part because she didn't want her parents to see her in prison orange. Somehow, she had to see her parents again. She had no idea where Aldo was, but she knew he must be in danger. She said a quiet prayer for him and hoped he would return soon.

"Trust me," Raj said. "Mr. Brink can handle anything."

CHAPTER 32

Just as a precaution, Aldo Brink drove forty-five miles west of Sam Hodge's home, after taking the unconscious Russian and throwing him into the trunk of his old blue Ford Taurus. It was a stock non-descript car, except for the modifications Brink made to the trunk. He'd fortified it from the inside. Having a captive break through the backseat would have been embarrassing he thought, so he made the modifications personally.

Fifty-five minutes after Brink's demand, the files he requested on Davis and Smith were sent to his cell phone. Brink pulled over, and after verifying the files, quickly connected the phone via USB cable to his tablet computer. Sixty seconds later, the files were downloaded.

Though they didn't have someone as adept as Taylor Ross, Brink took no chances that they might try to trace his location. He exited the car with the phone and wrapped a Velcro strap with magnet around it. Brink casually walked by a car stopped at a red light and attached it under the rear bumper. Seconds later, the car drove off into the night.

Have fun following that, Sam.

Brink drove off, turned right immediately, and headed north. He'd gone out of his way, but he figured it was better to be safe than sorry in case they were tracking his last known position. The journey would continue north for fifty miles. Brink needed some privacy to plan his next move and the underground safe house he established for himself six years ago would fit the bill perfectly. On the way, he pulled over once to inject the Russian with a special cocktail to keep him asleep.

The underground safe house couldn't be seen from a main road and had no road access, so when Brink pulled off, he took a dirt path that lead to a dead end and then just continued driving on the grass to a small clearing surrounded by dense trees. It was as secluded as possible, while still being close enough to civilization where he could get to and from it quickly and quietly.

Aldo Brink always considered things from all angles, and he knew the weak link in terms of secrecy when dealing with a hidden underground facility would be the builders. Brink couldn't build it himself, so naturally he needed to hire a company to do it. There were always non-disclosure agreements and things like that, and Brink would hire them under one of his false identities, but given how important it was, he wanted to remove the chance of the company records falling into the wrong hands, thus revealing his lair.

The individual workers could always talk, but Brink solved most of the problems by forming his own construction company under a false identity. Once formed, he hired workers who specialized in underground construction and "hired" his own company to build a data storage facility for a fictitious client. The project was halted by Brink when it reached what the workers thought was 75% completion, when in reality it met everything Brink wanted for himself.

He explained to the workers that the client, a data storage company, had gone bankrupt and would be unable to pay the remaining costs. Given that the construction company was a meager startup that struggled to attract new business and had been operating in the red for too long, Brink tearfully told his employees that he would be forced to declare the company bankrupt. This concluded his reign as a construction baron. The workers would remember where they built an underground facility, but they would end up at different companies going forward and would remember it as an unfinished project for a bankrupt company. They would never suspect what it would be used for. Afterwards, Brink planted more grass and made some additions himself. Today, the clearing looked like any unkempt piece of land you would find, a parcel filled with overgrown grass and weeds.

When his Ford Taurus entered the clearing, the underground sensors on the perimeter signaled to him that the coast was clear by sending a signal to his wristwatch that held a high power RF transmitter. It would only work if he was right next to it, but the transmitter was powerful enough to penetrate through the soil. Brink took off his watch so he could hold it in such a way that allowed him to push all four buttons at the same time.

The moment he pressed the buttons, the hydraulic lift went to work. A car-sized plot of grass moved downwards to a thirty degree angle creating a ramp. Brink drove down it, and continued for about fifty feet before parking next to his black BMW M3. The ramp returned to its original position, and thus totally concealed the entrance.

Though Brink blew up his house, he saw no reason to leave his BMW in the garage when it happened. The funny thing was Brink had read online in the local paper that the house exploded due to a gas leak while the owner had been away on vacation. No doubt the government was responsible for the newspaper getting that story, he thought. Brink still owned the land, and since no charges were pending against him, he thought he might come back to America one day with his wife and rebuild it. He buried that pleasant thought in the back of his mind and focused on the task at hand.

Brink opened the trunk and looked at the unconscious Russian. After hoisting him from the trunk, he dragged the smelly unconscious man down the hallway across the concrete floor to the main room. The space left no room for luxury. Everything had a purpose. It was utilitarian, and nothing more.

Brink chained the man to the floor and laid him on a cot. Next, he wheeled a medical cart over, and inserted an

IV into the Russian's arm. Brink didn't care if the man felt pain, but he needed him to stay alive for a while longer. Therefore, basic medical attention would be provided to him.

Once he finished, Brink moved to the desk where he reviewed the files Hodges sent him. He flipped through the digital files and noticed that both Gloria Smith and Mark Davis worked the Russian desk at the CIA before joining the no name unit. They were listed as off the grid officially, but Brink wasn't sure if he fully bought that.

Brink grabbed a bite to eat, put his blood stained clothes in the incinerator, and took a quick shower. After dressing in jeans and a black t-shirt, he saw the Russian starting to stir. Brink asked him some questions and the Russian seemed cooperative. It must have been all the drugs, he thought.

"What's your name?" Brink asked.

"Kozlov, Nikolai Kozlov."

Brink recognized the name immediately. The man he chained up in his underground bunker was the top enforcer for Anton Volodin. If an entry existed in the dictionary for a stereotypical burly Russian Mafioso, Nikolai's picture would certainly be there. "The Nikolai Kozlov?"

"Yes, I am him."

"The right hand man for Anton Volodin," Brink said. He glanced over where the Russian's right hand used to be. "Sorry, poor choice of words on my part."

The Russian looked upset at the comment, but only feigned some anger given his current state. "What do you want with me?" Kozlov asked. "Why not just kill me?"

"I want to meet your boss, and you're going to tell me where he is."

"Why?"

"Because I'm going to take you to him."

"Take my body to him, you mean," Nikolai said.

"Nope. I am going to deliver you to him alive. I want to meet him and discuss this business about blackmailing the President. I think he'll find our goals are not altogether different."

The Russian looked confused, but interested. "Why would you want to attack your own country like that?"

Brink moved in close. "Let's just say we've had a difference of opinion."

The drive to Atlantic City took almost two hours. Brink loved the feeling of being behind the wheel of his M3 again, though he would have preferred the trunk to be filled with luggage for a weekend trip with his fiancée, as opposed to an unconscious Russian hit man. After Kozlov gave up the location of his boss, Brink injected him again with a sleep agent and tossed him back into the reinforced plastic-lined trunk.

Anton Volodin owned a restaurant and bar downtown. Illegal gambling and prostitution were also part of the large establishment's amenities but somehow the authorities never made anything stick. Brink parked at the back alley door, and banged his clenched fist against it. "Special delivery!" A slot in the door slid open and a man's eyes peered out at Brink.

"No deliveries scheduled today. Piss off, before something bad happens to you."

"I think you will make an exception. I have something Anton Volodin will want."

"What could you have for him?" asked the doorman.

"Nikolai Kozlov. He's in my trunk."

"Bullshit."

Brink took a few steps back and clicked his trunk release. He reached down and pulled Kozlov's body up just enough so the doorman could see him. "I want to see Volodin, now."

The slot on the door slid shut and the doorman came to the alley to see Kozlov for himself. He yelled something in Russian and two other no neck Russians emerged. "Follow them," the doorman said as he pulled Kozlov from the car and closed the trunk. Brink locked the car and went inside.

They led Brink through the kitchen and into the main restaurant. As he passed the bar, numerous Russians gave him the evil eye. Brink assumed they were GRU agents posing as simple Mafia hoods. They didn't even frisk him, but Brink wasn't that surprised. These guys operated under the theory that if Brink pulled a gun and shot, at least one of them would be able to shoot him down. They had sized him up immediately as someone who wouldn't be interested in a suicide attack.

The C4 he taped to Nikolai before he pulled up in the alley, disagreed. *Just in case.*

If the Russians got too aggressive he would blow Nikolai to kingdom come with a simple push of a button on his watch. Naturally, Brink would try to be out of the blast radius when he did it, but if he had to be close, then that would be it. He didn't think it would come to it, but he never walked into a situation like this without a few tricks up his sleeve.

The restaurant was quite beautiful and must have cost a fortune, Brink thought. The bar was ornate, and everything from the carpet to the booze was top shelf. A dramatic staircase and balcony added to the grandeur of the room.

Brink knew Volodin wasn't stupid. He would at least hear what he had to say before ordering his men to shoot him. Brink had plans for that too, but he didn't think it would get that far. When he passed the bar, Brink saw Anton Volodin sitting in a corner booth smoking a cigar and drinking what he assumed was Russian vodka. Volodin waved the no neck Russians away and motioned for Brink to sit down.

Volodin was tall and fat, but not as fat as Brink figured he would be. He spoke with a voice obviously damaged by years of heavy tobacco use, and his face looked like it had been exposed to enough cigar smoke to kill most people. "Why do you wish to speak to me?" he asked.

"I think we have the same goals, and I know I'm in a position to help you achieve them."

Volodin saw Nikolai Kozlov helped into the room as a man attended to him. "What have you done to Nikolai? You cut off his hand!?"

"He's lucky I didn't cut off his head."

Volodin let out a large puff of smoke, and blew it into Brink's face. He took a drink and stared at him. "Why are you here?"

"I'm here because Nikolai Kozlov and your men tried to kill me. I don't like people trying to kill me."

"Nor do I. Before I ask who you are, what are you offering me?"

"I know your plans to blackmail the President have failed, and I know you are looking for payback. I will help you get it."

"Assuming I believe you, what do you want in return?" Volodin asked.

"I want you to help me find Mark Davis. I'm guessing you know who that is given how your plans went awry."

The expression on the grizzled Russian's face told Brink he knew exactly who Mark Davis was. But how, Brink wondered? He worked out of the embassy in Russia and GRU certainly monitored such things, so perhaps that explained it, he surmised.

"I know that name. From what I know, he had a hand in fouling up my plans," Volodin said as Brink chuckled a bit at another hand reference while Kozlov was just coming out of his stupor at the bar.

"Then our goals are even more in line than I thought," Brink said.

"So, who are you then?"

"He is Aldo Brink, and you should listen to him, father. He is the best there is at what he does."

The female voice came from behind them. As she descended the stairs in tight pants and a leather jacket, Brink instantly recognized Gloria Smith from her file photo.

"At last, you have returned to me," Anton said. The woman walked over and kissed the old Russian on the head. "This is my daughter, Gloria Volodin."

CHAPTER 33

He looked across the table, and sized her up. Brink listened carefully as Gloria Volodin vouched for him and convinced her father that he could be trusted. She explained how he had a bone to pick with the government and would have no problem striking the President. While Gloria appeared to speak to her father in a loving, respectful tone, Brink noticed something burning just below the surface. Behind every loving smile lay a twinge of anger on Gloria's face.

After Anton had been suitably placated, he suggested that Brink tell Gloria his plans to strike the government while he tended to other business. As Brink walked out of the room, he let Anton know about the C4 strapped to Nikolai. The old Russian gave a nod of respect to Brink's bold gambit.

It became clear to Brink that Anton Volodin trusted his daughter. Playing the perfect gentleman, Brink invited

Gloria to take a drive with him. He wanted to talk to her, but in an environment under his control. She gleefully accepted. Minutes later Brink was behind the wheel of his M3 driving west out of Atlantic City with the enigmatic Gloria Volodin in the passenger seat.

"Give me a reason not to shoot you in the head, and dump your body on the side of the road," Brink said.

Even though her life had just been threatened, Gloria Volodin couldn't stop smirking. She was well on her way to ingratiating herself to the one man she felt could handle her. The added element of danger just added to the pleasure she felt as she stared at his chiseled handsome face and dark Italian features. As she watched his strong hands grip the thick steering wheel, the image of Brink squeezing the life out of that weak incompetent fool Mark Davis sent another shiver through her body. "Is that your idea of sweet talk?" she asked.

Brink failed to see the humor in Gloria's question. "So how long have you been working for Volodin and GRU?"

"Many years, but you don't understand."

"What don't I understand?" Brink asked.

"It's true that I'm a GRU agent who successfully infiltrated the CIA, but that's the tip of the iceberg."

"I'm all ears."

"My father only thinks I infiltrated the CIA."

"So you're a double agent who penetrated GRU, is that it?"

"My father has treated me like property since I was a child. I was passed around and used. You can use your imagination. After the abuse I was trained to be the person you see now. He thinks I infiltrated the CIA, and I did, but my goal has nothing to do with harming the United States. I turned my back on my father years ago, and have been feeding Sam Hodges info on GRU."

The file that Hodges sent Brink discussed in detail Gloria's issues with men. She preferred using them and manipulating them to actually feeling for them. Brink also remembered Hodges mentioning something to him about how she had a "thing" for him. Brink didn't know exactly what that meant, but he knew she wasn't a normal woman.

"Lady, just whose side are you on?" Brink asked.

"The only side anyone should ever be on, their own!" Gloria yelled. "I learned from a young age that if you don't look out for yourself, no one will! You will be abused if you leave your life up to other people. You and your fiancée should know this better than anyone."

Brink slammed on the brakes and pulled the car over. He reached across and grabbed Gloria by the throat. "Play time is over," he said. "I know you and Mark Davis had something to do with the death of the Vice President and letting Jazlyn take the fall for it. You better say something worthwhile in the next ten seconds, or I will kill you right now."

The look on Gloria's face gave him pause. She was enjoying being strangled by him. Brink released his grip on her neck.

"Why do you think I warned you about Mark's attack in India? Why do you think I convinced Mark to dump Taylor at the hospital rather than kill him? I never wanted to hurt Jazlyn! Mark is out of control. He acted a week before he should have. We were assigned to kill the Vice President since my father and GRU were going to blackmail the President with damaging information. We had to make it look how we did so it wouldn't start a war between Russia and America. You must believe me. If I wanted you dead, why would I have warned you in India?"

"Where is Mark Davis?"

"He is going to contact me today or tomorrow, and I will set up a meeting. I will deliver him to you on a silver platter!"

"Good," Brink said. "So what's your endgame here?"

"I am going to help you do what you need to do. I owe you that much for what happened to Jazlyn."

"And?"

"And then I am going to make sure my father pays for what he's done. I have no allegiance to GRU, or the CIA. They are users, and I will never be used again."

Gloria felt confident that she had Brink under control, and worked hard to keep her feelings hidden. While Brink had a plan of his own, Gloria's was working too perfectly, she thought. Once Mark Davis was out of the way, she would earn Aldo's trust. Then, she would wait for an opportunity to remove Jazlyn from the equation, leaving her to pick up the shattered pieces of Aldo Brink's psyche. She didn't know how yet, but somewhere along the way an opportunity would present itself, and when it did, she would take it.

"So you want to help me?" Brink asked.

"Yes, I do." Gloria grabbed his hand tenderly.

Brink sensed something was amiss, but it didn't really matter. He wanted Mark Davis and if the double agent Gloria Volodin could assist him, he would use her. Brink had a plan of his own. He started the car and shot a wry smile at Gloria.

"OK," Brink said. "Prove it."

Later that evening, Gloria sat patiently with a glass of vodka on the rocks in one hand, and her cell phone in the other. Earlier, she had received a coded text message indicating her partner and lover Mark Davis would be calling any minute.

Across the room sat the man she hoped would be her greatest conquest. Infiltrating the CIA took years and an amazing level of discipline, but Aldo Brink posed an even greater challenge to her.

He looked relaxed in his chair, but Gloria knew what lurked below the surface of his cool exterior. He possessed the iron will of an uncompromising destroyer of anything that got in his way. Gloria had waited a lifetime to find a man like him, and here he sat in her Atlantic City high rise apartment.

Gloria adored great views, and her apartment had a great one of the city below. She especially enjoyed it at night, as the lights and passing cars brought the city to life. She looked at the casino nearby and smiled as she played her own version of Russian roulette. If she miscalculated, Brink would make her feel unimaginable pain. Unlike him, Gloria cared for no one. She felt life should be one giant gamble.

"You don't trust me, do you?"

"What gives you that idea?" Brink asked.

"The way you look at me."

"Trust is earned," Brink said. "Not given away."

When the phone rang, she looked at Brink and winked. "I told you he'd call," she said. Gloria put the phone on speaker, making sure Brink knew she had nothing to hide.

"Gloria, are you all right?" Mark asked.

"Yes, my love," Gloria said. "Where are you? I must see you."

"I'm at our place."

"Good, I am in my apartment in Atlantic City."

"Come as soon as you can. Make sure you aren't being followed."

Gloria winked at Brink again. "I can be there in ninety minutes. I have to take care of a few things first, so I'll be there tomorrow afternoon."

"Then we should leave the country together and stay out of sight until things calm down."

"With you, I will go anywhere."

The line went dead. Gloria smiled, crossed her legs, and sat back in her chair. Brink didn't look nearly as chipper. "Nicely done," he said. "You have my number. Call me when the meet is set."

Gloria's mind went into overdrive. Her heart raced. She didn't want him to leave.

Brink got up to leave but Gloria blocked his path. "We have about twelve hours to kill," she said. Her hand moved up towards his cheek. Brink snatched it by the wrist, and snarled.

"Not in a million years." He pushed her away forcefully and left the apartment, closing the door behind him. Gloria went back to her chair, crossed her legs, and took a drink.

"A lot sooner than that," she said.

CHAPTER 34

Nikolai Kozlov made sure he didn't follow too closely. He couldn't risk being seen. Gloria and Anton assured him that Brink was no threat, but he couldn't bear the thought of seeing the lovely Gloria gallivanting around with the man that cut off his hand. Nikolai grew up with Gloria, and though a few years older, had fallen in love with her many years ago. Naturally, he felt protective of her. Deep down he hated himself for not doing more to stop the abuse she suffered from her father and his gang of GRU Mafia. He would never let anything happen to her again, one hand or not.

Though he had made his feelings clear over the years, Gloria never reciprocated. With the exception of basic physical pleasure, she couldn't feel for anyone, not after what she endured as a young woman. Nikolai knew it, but he thought he could wear her down over time. Even with one hand, he had followed her and Aldo Brink just to make sure she stayed safe. Kozlov knew where the black BMW was headed. He had trailed Gloria before and found the house she visited. Staying behind Brink like this wouldn't work for long. Nikolai hated to admit it, but Brink was good, and would be able to spot a tail. For this reason, Nikolai hit the accelerator in his Mercedes and got to the house well ahead of them.

Not wanting to spook Mark, Brink dropped Gloria off two blocks from the house. Once she confirmed Mark was there, she would call him and discreetly let him know before luring her lover to a timely end. Brink wanted to barge right in, but the house they picked made that impossible. Mark would easily see Brink coming.

Brink watched from a distance as Gloria ventured up the sidewalk until she reached the house. The subdivision looked fairly new, and the homes were quite small and similar. Brink figured most of the suburbanites were at work for the day, because he could only see one other car, a Mercedes, parked on the street within eye distance. Brink was too far away to tell if anyone was in it.

Gloria readied her charms, and knocked. A moment later, Mark opened the door and welcomed her in. The second the door closed, she leapt into his arms.

"I missed you too," he said.

"Don't worry. I made sure I wasn't followed and I had the cab drop me off two blocks away at a different house."

"Smart girl."

"Are you ready to go?" Gloria asked. "I have supplies hidden that we can pick up, and then we can leave."

"We have money so we can buy anything we need. We shouldn't risk going anywhere else if we don't have to."

"My love, I need them. It will be quick, and then we will be out of here. Some place warm and romantic, I hope." Gloria kissed him and rubbed his chest with her perfectly manicured hands.

"I will do anything for you, Gloria. My bag is in the bedroom. I'll get it and we can leave. The car is in the garage."

Gloria's hand lingered on his chest as he pulled away to retrieve his bag. Soon, Mark would be out of her hair for good, and she would have earned some trust from her next attempted conquest, Aldo Brink.

She thought it would be over soon. Then she could turn her attention to more stimulating matters. All that changed when she saw a familiar man walking towards the house.

Nikolai couldn't take it anymore. He had watched the seductress walk to the house and enter, assuming she was meeting Aldo Brink for a romantic rendezvous away from the prying eyes of her father. How could she be spending time with the man who cut off his hand and killed their agents? She must be under duress, he thought.

As his hand squeezed the steering wheel in his Mercedes tighter with each passing minute, his blood boiled. He would kill the man that made him a cripple and show Gloria just what kind of man she had gotten mixed up with.

Nikolai exited the car, checked his pistol, and walked towards the house.

It was too late. Gloria tried desperately to think of something, but Mark spotted him too quickly. Nikolai must have followed her, she thought. *That idiot!*

Mark already had his pistol drawn. Gloria knew he would kill the Russian before he even got a shot off, but Nikolai turning up dead would only complicate her life right now, and she didn't need that. She had enough to deal with, she thought. Just as Mark squeezed the trigger, Gloria grabbed his arm and screamed for them to leave out the back while they still could. The bullet broke the glass in the front window, but missed its target. Nikolai returned fire.

"We have to go now! There could be more men outside!" Gloria screamed.

"We can't pick up your things now! We have to go! I'm sorry, Gloria."

She tugged at Mark's arm, dragging him to the garage as three more rounds whizzed past them. Gloria knew her plan had been blown up. Mark would never waste time going to pick up her fictitious belongings now. He would drive far away, and fast. She worried what Brink would think when he saw her and Mark driving away. He would undoubtedly think she had double crossed him.

Nikolai kicked in the front door and scanned the room. When he heard a car starting, he ran to the back, just in time to see Mark peel away in a dark grey Porsche Panamera. Nikolai had a shot and raised his pistol, but stopped when he saw Gloria in the passenger seat. He couldn't risk hitting her. Nikolai ran in vain to catch the fleeing car, and when he got back to his Mercedes he realized that for him, the chase was over. All four tires on his luxury sedan had been slashed.

He looked down the street and saw the Porsche driving away, with a black BMW speeding after it.

Brink didn't need Nikolai causing more trouble. If he had more time he would have disabled the car from under the hood, but in this instance slashing all four tires would be enough.

Mark drove the Porsche effortlessly as he weaved through traffic. Mark checked his rearview mirror and saw the man behind the wheel of the BMW that pursued him. Brink gestured with his right hand towards his eye, just as he did back in India. Mark jerked the wheel hard to the right and pulled onto the interstate.

Brink downshifted, sending the 414 horsepower under the hood into a monstrous growl. He easily followed Mark up the ramp to the interstate and closed the gap between them thanks to a heavy right foot. The road had three lanes, but given how the Porsche swerved in and out, it wasn't going to be wide enough. The Porsche pulled away as Mark's driving grew more reckless by the second.

When Brink checked his speedometer, it read 90 MPH. The fact that the Porsche had opened up a gap between them meant Mark must have been travelling well into triple digits. Brink remained calm. At the rate things were going, Mark wouldn't be able to keep up this pace for much longer. Traffic had been getting heavier, and the Porsche just missed hitting a semi-truck during an ill-advised lane change. Brink pushed the accelerator to the floor and pulled alongside the Porsche. They were approaching heavy traffic, and they would both have to slow down in a matter of seconds.

When he caught his eye, Mark looked a bit startled. Brink just smiled and pointed ahead, just before slamming on the powerful brakes of his BMW. His seatbelt saved him. Without it, Brink would have been ejected out the front windshield from the stopping power.

Gloria screamed for Mark to stop, but it was long past the point of no return. Mark hit the brakes, but it didn't matter. The Porsche slammed into the right rear of an SUV directly in front of them as Mark tried hopelessly to avoid it by turning the wheel.

The car lurched into a terrifying spin and smashed into another car as an unstoppable chain reaction began. When the squealing of rubber subsided, all that was left were the screams of injured motorists and the stubborn sound of a car horn that blared continuously.

A dazed Gloria looked to her left, and saw an empty seat. She felt someone's strong hands pulling her from the car. When her blurred vision corrected itself, she wasn't sure if she should be happy or terrified that Aldo Brink was her rescuer.

Brink looked up and saw Mark running down an exit ramp. He could have given chase, but remained content to bring Gloria back to the safety of his BMW. The people who put Jazlyn into this Hell deserved to die, but a simple bullet to the head didn't fit the crime. He had to torment him first. Shooting him now wouldn't be justice at all.

Brink would deal with Mark Davis, and knew exactly how he would do it.

CHAPTER 35

After arriving at his home in Panaji, Soham Gupta took a quick shower and grabbed a bite to eat. Though he willingly joined the righteous battle brought to him by his friend Aldo Brink, his billion dollar business interests still needed attention. He had been away from home visiting Europe, discussing a handful of ventures that involved convincing other wealthy businessmen to bring investment capital to India. Soon enough, he would know how successful the trip had been, but right now there were more important matters at hand.

Jazlyn Reyes was his responsibility until Aldo returned. He regretted having to leave her here with Raj, but it couldn't be helped. Now, he cleared his schedule and would be around to keep her company as long as she needed it.

After finding the door to her room open, he peeked inside. The bed was neatly made, and a few of her personal items were seen throughout the room. "Must be outside or in the living room," he said. The weather was gorgeous and she must have had her fill of being cooped up inside by now.

Soham moved to the living room, but found nothing, except for a staff member tidying up. His pace quickened as he checked the kitchen, and the adjoining balcony. He quickly walked down the nearby steps and onto the beautiful grounds that were kept in perfect condition by a dedicated staff of groundskeepers.

Scanning the lush grounds for a moment kept his heart pounding, but relief came when Raj emerged from the behind the mango trees. The relief didn't last as the expression on Raj's face told Soham almost everything he needed to know.

"Thank God you are back," Raj said. "Sir, something terrible has happened."

Having left the scene of the accident, Aldo Brink drove for a few miles, and then pulled off the main road to a wooded area where he exited the car and walked around to the passenger side. Brink didn't know it, but his plan was seconds away from having to take a major detour. The phone call he received made that clear.

"Aldo, its Soham," said the Indian, as if Brink wouldn't immediately recognize his old friend's voice.

"I'm a little busy right now, so please make it quick," Brink said as he looked at the still groggy Gloria Volodin in the passenger seat of his BMW.

"It's an emergency. I don't know how to tell you this, but…"

"Just tell me."

"Jazlyn is gone."

"What!?"

"She just left on her own. She left Raj a note. It said she had to do something important and that she would be back very soon. Then it said we shouldn't worry. That was it. I assume the new identity you gave her is rock solid, and with her new hair color, she should be able to avoid getting picked up."

"By the authorities, yes," Brink said.

"What do you mean?" Soham asked.

"Nothing, I will find her. Just be ready for my call."

"Anything you need. My jet is standing by for you. It is still in Washington and ready when you need it."

"Thanks, Soham."

"Good luck, my friend."

The line went dead. Brink almost threw his phone down in anger, but thought better of it. After pacing for a few moments, he walked to the car, opened the door, and dragged Gloria out by her hair. He slammed the car door behind her, and pushed her up against it. She started to come around, but Brink slapped her across the face to speed up the process.

"If anything happens to her," Brink said. He drew his knife and held it against Gloria's cheek. "I will turn your pretty little face into a jigsaw puzzle."

"What? What happened?" Gloria asked.

"You put her in this situation, so I am holding you responsible."

Brink threw her to the ground, and got behind the wheel of his BMW.

"I can help you!" Gloria screamed as Brink pushed the start button. "I will get my father to help find her! I can help, damn you!"

Brink lowered the window and tossed her cell phone at her feet. "I know where she is, you dumb bitch." He sped off in a cloud of dust, leaving Gloria to walk or hitchhike back to Atlantic City.

Jazlyn knew the danger. She wasn't a fool. Aldo would be furious, but she had to do what she had to do. If anyone would understand that, he would. It would be a quick visit, but a necessary one.

The streets of Miami were just as she remembered them, vibrant and alive. She felt as though she had been away for years. Her confinement made her appreciate every smell and color that filled the air. She could almost taste the beach. While her senses went into overload, she quickly refocused and turned towards the house her parents bought a few years ago.

She had many great memories growing up. Her parents worked hard to give her a chance to be a success, and she couldn't live with the thought of not seeing them again. She took a deep breath and walked slowly down the sidewalk towards the colorful house. It looked like the perfect place to retire for her mom and dad, she thought.

Jazlyn never saw it coming. Perhaps the thought of seeing her parents after all that had happened made her less aware of her surroundings than usual. She assumed the arm around her throat belonged to a man, but she couldn't see for sure. As she tried to scream, a rag was put over her mouth and nose that muffled her cries for help. Jazlyn fought with all her might, and tried to reach up to the eyes of her attacker. Before she could reach them she felt her body getting tired. Jazlyn started to pass out. With only seconds to think, she knew it must have been something on the rag.

She heard a vehicle pull up, and what sounded like a van door slide open. The next sensation she felt was pain when she hit her head as she was thrown into the van. She felt like she was about to pass out, but before she did, someone from behind cuffed her hands and blindfolded her. As she nodded off, she could hear the van driving away, and a few men talking in a language she recognized, but didn't understand.

CHAPTER 36

S oham's jet darted through the clouds. Inside, Brink sat stoically. He always pictured going back to Florida to visit Jazlyn's family, but he thought it would be to celebrate their engagement. Even without the safeguards he put in place, Brink knew she must have gone back home. The fact that she never let her parents see her while in prison had eaten away at her. She understood that it was a horrible thing for her to do, and she couldn't live with it one second longer.

Aldo Brink left very little to chance in his life. Ironically, letting Jazlyn into it was the biggest chance he ever took. He checked his smart phone and the GPS dot hadn't moved since he boarded Soham's jet. The day after he rescued Jazlyn from prison, Brink slipped the engagement ring back onto her finger, just as he did months earlier at the arboretum.

"Promise me something," he said.

"Anything."

"Promise me you will always keep it on."

To be sure, there were loving words behind his request, but Aldo Brink had an ulterior motive. While planning her escape, he had the ring altered to conceal a state of the art GPS tracker powered by both light and the kinetic energy of a person's daily movements. It had been a project of Taylor Ross' and he offered it to Aldo when he asked the techno whiz for advice on what to use. The technology inside the ring turned out to be more expensive than the jewelry itself. Brink did the same thing to her favorite necklace and anklet. He figured she would always have at least one of them on.

He wasn't the type to be possessive and spy on his future wife, but their particular situation called for extraordinary measures. He would only use it if he genuinely feared for her life. Once the threat to them passed, he would have it removed. As long as the danger persisted, he needed a way to know her location if anything bad happened. She wouldn't like the idea of being tracked in such a way, but Aldo was willing to accept her wrath on the matter if it meant her safety. He only intended it to be a short term thing anyway, while he dealt with the immediate threats to her. In any case, he didn't think she would mind being tracked by him, if it meant being rescued, again.

While not a religious man, Brink said a prayer at forty thousand feet that Jazlyn still wore her jewelry. He didn't know her condition, and while he hoped for the best, he feared the worst. With some luck he would walk into the

Reyes' house, and find Jazlyn having a cup of coffee with her parents. If so, they would promptly say goodbye and contact them again as soon as possible. Brink knew any competent adversary would be watching Jazlyn's parents' house in the hope she would somehow make contact with them, either by phone or in person. They probably had the house bugged for sound and video as well.

His hopes of a positive outcome were quickly dashed when his phone rang. At the moment he carried two phones. The first was his one of many encrypted smartphones that he used to communicate with Soham, the Harrison brothers, and anyone else he trusted with his life. His second phone was a throw away that he had been using for the past forty-eight hours or so for his dealings with Gloria and the Russians. The ringing came from the throw away.

"What do you want?" Brink asked.

"I tried to tell you, I want to help you!" Gloria said. "Trust me; you are going to want to hear what I have to say."

"Speak."

"My father's people have her."

Brink stood up from his seat, took a breath, and paced up and down the aisle. "Where?" he asked.

"Miami. They grabbed her and brought her to his estate on Star Island."

Brink gritted his teeth. He knew from the tracker Gloria was telling the truth about Florida. He needed to keep his options open in case Jazlyn's jewelry had been separated from her already, or in the future. If so, Gloria would be his best lead to tracking her down.

"It's a gated community," she said. "There is an armed guard at the bridge entrance, so unless you want to get wet and reach the house that way, you will have to deal with him."

"I can do that."

"Of course you can, but when someone discovers the guard is gone or sees his body, they will call the police and the whole place will be swarmed in minutes. You need me to keep him busy so you can get to the house without any commotion."

Brink let her think she had provided him a great option. "OK Gloria, let's do it," Brink said. "If you double cross me, I will kill you." He expected her to try and stick a knife in his back at some point, but couldn't be sure when.

"We will get her back. I promise you."

"Never make a promise you can't keep, Gloria."

"You still don't trust me? You will when you see me help you get her back."

"Where are you?" Brink asked.

"I am on a plane headed to Miami. I assume you are flying there as we speak, but if not, you need to get there fast. I will contact you when I land. She is currently being held in the guest house of the property, and I will make sure she hasn't been moved before you are ready to go."

Brink hung up the phone. He didn't like it. How could he? There were too many variables here that he couldn't account for. Volodin and GRU must have had a reason for grabbing her. It could be as simple as retribution for mucking up their plan of blackmail. Brink knew GRU to be ruthless and calculating, so anything was possible.

They would kill and torture her just to send a message even though it wasn't Jazlyn's fault she got mixed up in this. Brink also knew something else could be going on. Perhaps they had something special in mind for her.

In the end, the why was irrelevant. He had to get Jazlyn out of there, now.

She couldn't help but snicker at the irony. Jazlyn had escaped from one prison, only to be confined in another. Her new digs were quite a bit nicer than the Wilson Prison Complex though. While she didn't know exactly where, the décor of the room looked to be typical Miami.

When one of her captors opened a door to leave, the sounds she heard made her almost positive that she was still in the city where she grew up. She could hear sounds of boats passing on the water. Was she on the beach or the Intracoastal Waterway? She couldn't tell, but she must still be in Miami, she thought.

Her captors had removed her blindfold as soon as they tied her to the chair, in what looked like the living room of a very nice house. She had seen the faces of at least three of her captors, and they seemed totally at peace with this fact.

This meant one thing to Jazlyn. They were going to kill her anyway, so it didn't matter that she could identify them later.

She had no formal training for these kinds of situations and worked out of an office most of the time. Aldo had given her a few basic classes in self-defense, and she cursed herself for not taking it more seriously at the time.

While she failed her first test in self-defense, Aldo had also taught her something else. He taught her the basics of always being aware of your surroundings and to always take inventory of what you see and hear, because you never know how it might be useful later. The second Jazlyn awoke in this lavish prison; she did as she was taught.

One of her captors entered the room after shouting something in Russian to another man. The man walked over to her and promptly slapped her across the face. Her cheek throbbed with pain, but Jazlyn did an admirable job of maintaining a tough exterior. She wouldn't let him see her pain.

She said nothing, and wasn't about to give the Russian any satisfaction by breaking down and crying.

"That is for trying to scratch my eyes out, you bitch!" The Russian paced back and forth. "We have big plans for you. The news got it all wrong you see. You are a deep cover GRU agent who will die in the glorious service of Russia as you assassinate the President. Of course we will deny all knowledge, but the people in Washington will remember forever that you never go back on a deal with GRU."

Her eyes darted around hopelessly looking for some escape. She might not have had a chance when tied up, but she promised herself that if given the chance, she would fight for her life with everything she could muster. After all she had been through; she resolved to make sure her life ended honorably, even if she would be the only one on Earth who knew it.

Jazlyn barely understood what the burly Russian had just said to her, but she knew it couldn't be good.

Aldo, where are you?

CHAPTER 37

Gloria Volodin took a deep breath. As she watched Aldo Brink approach the property, she finished covering up the body of the security guard. Moments before, she'd distracted the young man with her feminine wiles. The poor guy let his hormones get the best of him. The moment he dropped his guard, Gloria injected him with a sleep agent. He wasn't GRU, and Brink told her to make sure he wasn't permanently harmed. In a few hours he would wake up, and be no worse for wear. Gloria slipped into his official looking security guard shirt and casually waved to homeowners coming and going.

Now, she acted as lookout for Aldo Brink's rescue mission. While that was the plan she agreed to, Gloria had a twist of her own that she planned to unleash. She knew she might never get another chance as good as this, so it had to work. The timing would be critical.

Brink reached the perimeter of the estate. It had a classic, yet colorful look to it. It had to be worth well into ten figures, he thought. He had no idea what the inside would look like, but he planned on redecorating it with a heavy dose of Russian brain matter grey. Brink stalked his first target. The guard at the front driveway gate had no idea he was about to die.

Quietly, the knife sliced across the Russian's throat. His killer had crept up behind him without making a sound. After quickly wiping the blade of his knife, Brink sheathed it and moved towards the guest house. His eyes scanned the windows and detected no movement inside the main house. Brink readied his pistol. The thick black suppressor screwed into the end of the barrel quickly and quietly. He stayed low, allowing the bushes to give him some cover as he approached.

He stood mere feet from the front door. Seconds later, the door opened slowly. In the blink of an eye Brink crept inside, without making a sound.

The sound of an interrogation filled the air. Auditory clues instantly gave away Jazlyn's location. Brink had to keep his head. He wanted to storm into the room where Jazlyn was being held and kill them all, but that would be suicide. Securing his flanks had to take priority, or he risked being ambushed upon reaching her. Therefore, he had to take out a few more sentries before reuniting with his soul mate.

Luckily, the building's massive size gave him plenty of room to maneuver. The ranch style guest house had an impressive amount of square footage under roof, but only had one bedroom. While the spaces were limited in number, their size gave Brink plenty of angles to ply his trade. The black ops agent didn't have to wait long. After sizing up the foyer, Brink quickly moved right into the dining area. A Russian turned to face him, and was greeted by the long barrel of Brink's HK45. The Russian calmly put his hands up in surrender.

"Do what I say or you're dead," Brink growled quietly.

"OK," grunted the Russian.

"Yell as loud as you can into your radio, we have an intruder and a man down in the dining room."

"You will just shoot me."

"I promise I won't shoot you."

The Russian let out a deep breath before clicking his radio button. "We have an intruder and a man down in the dining room!"

Seconds later two Russians stormed into the room, but saw nothing. They moved towards the swinging kitchen door, their guns trained straight ahead as sweat poured from their brows.

A voice cried out. "The American is in the kitchen!"

The kitchen door burst open and the two Russians opened fire at the figure charging through. Their fear made them react more quickly than their brains should have allowed. The hail of bullets eviscerated their comrade who had been standing guard in the dining room. Realizing what they had done, they crept closer to the body of their dead friend who now resided in a pool of his own blood on the dining room floor. The two Russians didn't have long to mourn. A subsonic bullet struck each of them in the back of the head. They fell to the floor right next to the man whom they had gunned down moments earlier. Brink quickly checked to make sure they were dead, and continued to the left side of the house.

You can't trust anyone in this business.

The remaining Russians were in a panic. They checked the house, but found nothing. The GRU agents raced back to the living room, where they had left Jazlyn bound and gagged. Now, they found her standing alone in the middle of the room with a blank expression on her face.

"What are you doing!?" the lead Russian asked. Silence followed.

Jazlyn only had to stay still for a few more seconds for the plan to work. The poor girl's nerves were obviously frayed, and her darting eyes betrayed Aldo's plan to her Russian captors. Brink had left Jazlyn there for a few seconds as a decoy so he could flank the overly aggressive Russians and take them out. All it took was a quick glance from Jazlyn that gave away Aldo's position. The Russians knew they had walked into a trap.

A flash of light accompanied by a thunderous boom filled the room just as the five Russians were turning to see their stalker. Had Jazlyn not glanced behind them, all five would have felt the full force of the flash bang grenade that Brink expertly tossed at their feet. The lead Russian avoided it and lunged forward taking Jazlyn down, ironically sparing her from the disorientation the remaining four Russians were feeling at this very moment. Brink fired four quick shots from fifteen feet down the hallway. The four disoriented Russians were dead before they even knew what had blinded them in the first place.

Brink took one step forward toward the living room, when he felt someone coming up from behind him. He spun around catching the attacking Russian's outstretched arm, and pushed it in a direction where his pistol could do no harm. One quick move from Brink, and the Russian's wrist stood at the breaking point. With no choice, the burly man dropped his pistol, and shoved Brink with all his might into the living room. Aldo's mind quickly flashed to the drills he used to run back during high school football practice as he and the man crashed against the living room wall.

Out of the corner of his eye, Brink could see Jazlyn and the lead Russian struggling on the floor. His fiancée was giving it all she had, and had gotten a few good shots in on her captor. Brink had to get rid of this burly Russian, now. As the Russian held him against the wall, Brink unsheathed his knife and drew it with his right hand. A second later, the knife had plunged into the man's throat. He fell to the ground, hopelessly clutching his wound.

Brink turned, and saw the last Russian holding Jazlyn at knifepoint. The black ops agent calmly wiped the blood from his knife and sheathed it on his thigh. He took a quick glance and saw where his pistol had fallen during the scuffle. It resided on the floor a few feet away, and Brink made a mental note of its exact position. He walked toward

Jazlyn in a manner that suggested he didn't have a care in the world.

The Russian grinned as he stroked Jazlyn's throat with his knife. He sensed that he had the American in a box. As long as he had his woman at knifepoint, he wouldn't be able to do anything. If he had a gun, it would be different, but the American found himself unarmed after dispatching the rest of the Russian captors moments ago.

"Try anything, and your woman gets her throat cut!" the Russian screamed.

"I won't try anything," Brink said. "Just make sure you've thought this through." Brink took one step forward and stopped.

"Don't move, or she dies!"

"OK, kill her."

"What!? Ha, you see, he doesn't even care about you!"

Jazlyn shot daggers at her fiancé, as the look on her face went from bad to worse. *What the Hell are you doing, Aldo?*

"Think it through, comrade. Only way out of this house is out that door, and that means you have to move with her past me, and we both know if you get close to me I am going to take that knife away from you and then....well you know what happens next."

Brink crossed his arms and spoke in a matter of fact tone. "Of course, you could kill her, but then it would be just you, me, and your knife. You saw what I just did to your friends here, so what do you think I will do to the man who killed her?"

The Russian didn't like where this was going. His eyes began to dart from side to side looking for some escape. He hadn't thought this through at all, just like the American said. His breath became rapid, which Brink noticed immediately as he continued his soliloquy.

"You could throw the knife at me, but chances are you will miss and then I will have your knife." Brink saw the Russian look down at a nearby pistol dropped from one of his Russian friends. "You could lunge for the gun, but you don't have any idea if it's loaded or empty, and the second you reach for it I am going to reach for you, break both your arms, and beat you to death with that very gun."

"I don't fall for your games!" the Russian screeched.

"Want to know what happens next?"

"I will kill her! I swear I will!"

"I know, I know. You are a tough guy who kills innocent women, I get it. I'm very afraid. Ya know, I've just decided not to kill you right away. After you slit her throat, I am going to take you to a special place."

"Special place?"

"Oh, yes. You will absolutely hate it. I am going to strap you down to a metal table and let you experience pain you never thought possible. I will cut off your fingers, arms, and legs, in that order. First though, I will cut out one of your eyes, leaving you with one left to see what I am doing to you. That's just the beginning."

"You're crazy!"

"So, go ahead and kill her, but think it through. The best case for you is a quick death in this room after you do it, while the worst is a field trip to my special place. Either way, you better choose soon before I choose for you. You have exhausted my patience."

"If you were me, what would you do?" The Russian asked, looking more terrified than Jazlyn.

"Run," Brink said.

The Russian looked left to the window. He took a breath and shoved Jazlyn forward towards Brink as he ran to it. As Brink caught the woman he loved, the Russian made a desperate lunge toward the window, shoulder first with his arms shielding his face. The hefty Russian bounced off the window and landed on the floor with a tremendous thud. It wasn't an ordinary window as the GRU agent assumed, but an incredibly thick piece of ballistic glass capable of stopping a .357 magnum. Anton Volodin took his security seriously, it appeared.

Brink kissed Jazlyn on the forehead, before moving toward the Russian who had risen to his feet. He brandished the knife and waved it at Brink who stood stoically within arm's length. "Well?" Brink asked.

The Russian lunged forward with the knife, attempting to stab Brink in the neck. The Russian's wrist entered a vice grip by the time it reached the half-way point to its intended target. In a flash, Brink had caught the Russian's wrist with his right hand, and with his left was turning the man's arm back towards him. One more surge of energy from both of Brink's hands and the knife that had been meant for him, stabbed into the Russian's neck as his own hand still grasped it. The Russian fell, while the luxurious carpeting struggled to absorb the blood pouring from his neck.

Brink turned around, picked up his pistol, and quickly walked towards Jazlyn. He took her hand and led her out the front door of the guest house, before stopping to think better of it.

"Stay here for a second," he said.

He raced out of the house leaving Jazlyn in the doorway. He quickly scanned the area, looking for a possible ambush or any GRU backup that might have arrived. Brink was just about to turn and motion for Jazlyn to come to him when he heard something ominous. It would have been imperceptible to anyone else, but when he heard it he knew what would come next.

He sprinted towards Jazlyn and screamed for her to run away from the house, but it was too late.

Jazlyn ran from the doorway towards her fiancé, but inexplicably turned to look back, just as it exploded behind her. The concussive force pushed her forward and into Brink's arms. He caught her and shielded her with his body from most of the flames thanks to his fire resistant tactical clothing.

They both felt the blast, but because of how their bodies ended up being oriented to the explosion, Jazlyn absorbed the majority of it. She laid face down in the driveway and wasn't moving.

Brink looked at the house. Remarkably, it looked to be in good shape. The guest house was untouched except for the doorway. The bomb apparently was designed to just decimate the entryway, and not destroy the whole house.

After turning her over, Brink's blood boiled when he got a look at Jazlyn's beautiful face.

CHAPTER 38

Gloria planted the explosives at the guest house entryway before Brink even arrived. He did exactly what she knew he was capable of. He had dispatched some more of her father's best men, and now had a fiancée with a disfigured face.

Brink quickly spirited Jazlyn away after the blast. Gloria hadn't seen them since the explosion, but Brink called her the next day to let her know they made it out alive, but that Jazlyn had horrible burns to her face and hands, along with a busted knee.

Gloria feigned concern in a performance worthy of an Academy Award, as she knew it was only a matter of time before Aldo Brink dumped his hideous girlfriend. How could a man like that be with someone like her, now?

She laid it on thick, and blamed it all on her father. The same father whom she hated from childhood. That part was actually true, which made the overall lie more believable.

Of course, Gloria had aimed to kill Jazlyn in the explosion, but this worked just as well. It made the whole thing even more macabre, and for Gloria Volodin, that meant something. Now, Gloria would simply wait. She knew Brink still needed to kill Mark Davis, and she would be happy to help him do so.

Inside the cabin of Soham's jet, Aldo Brink paced up and down the aisle. They were streaking across the Atlantic, when Brink turned on the TV to see a Miami news report on a multiple homicide and explosion on Star Island. He would make Anton Volodin pay for this treachery. His concern now rested solely with the love of his life. He blamed himself, of course.

"How could I be so stupid?" he asked himself. "Only a fool would think a guy like me could have a wife."

It wasn't his fault that she got involved in all of this, but he blamed himself for leaving her alone in India. Had he stayed with her the entire time, she never could have run off to Florida, never would have been captured, and never would have...Brink stopped himself.

He couldn't think like that, and he knew it. Nothing could change what happened, so now he had to move forward. Thankfully, staying focused in the face of incredible stress was part of what made Aldo Brink special.

As always, he had a plan. From the second he picked Jazlyn up after the blast, he knew what he had to do. His plan was grotesque, but he had no choice. Jazlyn deserved to be free from looking over her shoulder for the rest of her life. She deserved better than that. He loved her no matter what, but this situation made things impossible.

Brink hadn't seen him in years, but if anyone could help with his cruel yet necessary plan of action, it would be him. After dropping Jazlyn off with Soham, Brink would show up on his doorstep, and call in his marker.

CHAPTER 39

Strom Metzger walked through his home in Stuttgart, Germany, sat by his fireplace, and sipped red wine from an odd looking glass. The home had a modern, but disturbingly sterile feel to it. Contemporary walls with a heavy dose of hard light unnerved most visitors when they entered. The living area looked suitable for a mortician's client. Cold slabs of concrete and steel serving as tables added to the odd décor. Much like the man who resided there, it was hard to look at. Strom, 57, stood a razor thin 6'4 and wore tight fitting clothes at all times. His thin reddish lips took another sip when the front doorbell rang.

He walked slowly to the security camera monitor. Had his skin not been the palest shade of white year round already, the sight of the man at his front door most assuredly would have turned it that way.

Strom recognized Aldo Brink immediately. He thought for a moment about racing to get his gun, but thought better of it. There would be no point in such a foolish endeavor. If Aldo Brink wanted him dead, he wouldn't be ringing the doorbell like a civilized person. Strom knew first hand that Aldo Brink was not a man to mess around with. His boney finger pressed the button on the wall panel and buzzed him in.

"Come in," Strom said into the speaker. "Join me in the living room by the fire."

Though he heard it through the speaker and not in person, Brink recognized Strom's distinct voice. The man still spoke with an unsettling hiss, which Brink had heard before.

A moment later, Brink strolled into the living room and sat across the coffee table from his old acquaintance. Strom's face had a taut and unnatural look to it. His skin looked like it had been pulled back over and over in a desperate attempt to look young. He only had three or four total strands of hair Brink thought, and they looked to be glued on across the top of his massive pale white head. Octagonal eyeglasses completed his look.

"What brings you to my humble home?" Strom asked.

"This place looks like a morgue."

"We all have our tastes, don't we?"

Brink cringed as those red lips hissed and took another sip of wine. "I have a patient for you. She is a very important woman to me."

Strom's eyes lit up. "A female patient, you say? How lovely."

For the last twenty-five years, Strom Metzger had worked as a successful surgeon. His skill in the operating room had made him fabulously wealthy, but the money gave him no joy. He viewed himself as a master sculptor. He lived to carve up human flesh and make a masterpiece.

The catch was that he only did this for criminals, preferably criminals with the means to pay his massive fee. In turn, they would get a new face, or whatever else they needed to avoid detection. Sometimes, his job was as simple as removing a bullet from the shoulder of someone who had an unfortunate encounter with the police. He had given Middle East terrorists completely new faces. Afterwards, the terrorists could blend right in with the WASPS in Greenwich, Connecticut.

Strom loved to use his talents on everyone, but he especially enjoyed the female patients since he had so few of them. Most evil people with means were men, of course. What a pity, he thought.

"You are one creepy son of a bitch," Brink said.

"So, who is this woman?"

"Her." Brink pulled a picture from his inside jacket pocket and slid it across the coffee table. Strom picked it up and stared at it for an inordinate amount of time. His breath quickened the longer he looked at it.

"She is beautiful and exotic. I would love to work on her."

"Good."

"What a shame to alter such a pretty face, though," Strom said.

"I need you to make her into a different person, so the authorities would never recognize her by a quick glance."

Strom put the picture in his pocket, took a sip of wine, and exhaled a deep breath. "I can do that."

"And?"

"I need some time to gather the appropriate provisions."

"How long?" Brink asked.

"Not long at all. Forty-eight hours maximum. I also require payment, of course."

"Two million dollars, if I remember your rate correctly."

"Yes, but for you, one million. I owe you for looking the other way all these years, and because it is a woman."

Brink stood up. "Good, I will wire you the money and will deliver her to you in a few days with all the final details." Strom nodded and Brink walked towards the door, before turning back. "Strom, I never looked the other way. I used you to track down the very people I was looking for. If I took you out, then I wouldn't know where they would go for help. You are only alive, because I've allowed you to live."

"Quite right," Strom said.

Brink left the house and drove away, while Strom sat by his fireplace. It all made sense to him now. For years he had seen a few of his clients wind up dead even after their procedures. He had wondered how they could be so stupid. In turns out they weren't stupid. Aldo Brink had been too smart. Strom didn't mind. Brink could kill every single one

246

of them for all he cared, as long as new canvases arrived for him to work on. He pulled the picture from his pocket, and took another long look.

See you soon, my lovely.

CHAPTER 40

Brink dreaded telling Jazlyn that she needed surgery, but he would cross that bridge when he came to it. He still had to worry about Mark Davis, traitors in the American government, and the Russian GRU agents who were trying to kill them. Those problems needed to be addressed, and fast.

He placed a call to Gloria, and asked her to meet him at the Casino Prestige. With Jazlyn in her current state, he needed to see Gloria, now. He told her that Jazlyn needed surgery, and in the end it would be the best thing for everyone. Brink had a twinge of sadness in his voice when he spoke. So much so, that he knew Gloria picked up on it.

When Gloria hung up the phone, a delicious smile graced her face. She knew Brink wouldn't just throw himself at her feet and beg for it, but she could sense he was ripe for the kill. His fiancée lay disfigured, and all he had left was a desperate Hail Mary attempt to restore the face he had fallen in love with to its former beauty. Brink needed her now more than ever, she thought. No one else could help him eliminate the threats that dogged him, and no one else could provide the companionship that she so eagerly wished to give.

The last thing Brink told her on the phone was how he looked forward to thanking her in person. You didn't need ESP to read between those lines, Gloria thought. The possibilities were so intoxicating, she could barely sit still. Soon, she would rendezvous with the man, the killer of her dreams, to embark on an adventure with him worthy of a major motion picture.

She felt no remorse for the plight of Jazlyn Reyes. It served the bitch right for trying to marry a man like Aldo Brink, Gloria thought. He needed someone just like himself. In other words, he needed Gloria. The daughter of the notorious Anton Volodin let all these thoughts flow through her mind and body as she lay on her luxurious bed. Over the next few days she would help Aldo Brink dispose of Mark Davis, her father, and anyone else who stood in their way.

CHAPTER 41

Jazlyn Reyes felt considerable pain as she lay in bed. Fortunately for her, the only thing that could possibly brighten her spirits walked through the bedroom door and pulled up a chair next to her. Aldo had returned.

She took the news of the surgery surprisingly well. Brink wondered if his fiancée was just too exhausted both mentally and physically to put up any resistance. He silently cursed himself for putting her through this ordeal.

Raj, Soham's trusted servant had spent hours applying an ancient Indian balm on Jazlyn's burns. She said it helped considerably, and thanked Raj profusely for everything he had done for her. As always, the modest Indian said he felt honored to assist such a lovely woman. When Brink walked in, Raj excused himself.

"How are you feeling, Jaz?" Brink asked.

"I just can't take this anymore, but I am much better now that you're here."

"I am so sorry about all this."

"Sorry for saving my life? Sorry for saving me from a life behind bars? Yeah, you're a real jerk."

Brink leaned down and kissed her on the forehead. "I love you," he said.

"I love you too."

"I was so proud of you at the house. You fought with everything you had. That Russian was lucky I got to him before you finished him off."

"Why thank you," Jazlyn said.

"I know this whole ordeal has been a living Hell for you, but my admiration for you has only grown during it."

"It has?"

"You handled all of this with more grace than anyone ever could."

"Yeah, well, you didn't see me in prison crying myself to sleep at night. I don't think I can go on like this. Maybe I should stop this whole thing and turn myself in?"

"Jaz, I promise you, it will all be over soon, and you will never have to fear for your life again."

As grotesque as it was, Aldo Brink had a plan.

CHAPTER 42

The Casino Prestige sliced through the Bay of Bengal with ease. The massive ocean liner had been converted into a luxurious hotel and casino shortly after the Indian government loosened restrictions on gambling.

For many years, gambling was restricted in India. The restrictions were so severe that they became a de facto ban. As the economy grew, and tourism skyrocketed, important business interests asked that at least a few casinos be allowed. Just like in the USA, the politicians did an end run around the issue and said that casinos could operate on the water. In America, there were riverboats, and in the Bay of Bengal off the Indian coast, sailed the Casino Prestige.

Aldo Brink walked forcefully into the main gaming area of the ship. The clientele on board dressed exquisitely, and Aldo did the same. His dark Zegna suit fit him perfectly. When he walked across the casino floor, he scanned the room for threats. If he did so consciously it might have grown into a nuisance for him, but at this stage of his career it had evolved into an automatic response that he didn't even notice anymore. He was fully aware of how often this habit had saved his life, however.

He moved swiftly to the back wall of the gaming area where he took a seat at a reserved VIP table. The dealer bowed his head, welcoming Aldo to the table. "Gambling alone tonight, sir?" the dealer asked.

"No, my companion should be here any minute."

Across the room, almost on cue, Gloria emerged from the elevator. The moment she stepped onto the gaming floor, all eyes focused on her. She didn't look the part of a cold-blooded double agent. Her silver dress sparkled under the lights of the gaming floor and hugged her body in just the right places. Gloria caught Brink's eye as she seductively sauntered across the room and joined him at the VIP table. The professional card dealer and server bowed his head welcoming the lady, and pulled a dark satin curtain giving the VIP's complete privacy from curious onlookers. "Good evening. I am honored to be your dealer and personal valet for the evening," he said.

Gloria moved sensually to the table and sat down. She crossed her legs seductively in an effort to entice him, revealing the rose tattoo on her ankle.

"Though I was heartbroken to hear the news about Jazlyn, I am glad you called me. I know we can fix the problem, together," Gloria said.

"Nothing is impossible," Brink said.

"You play Chemin de Fer, I see."

"Yes, it is a favorite of mine," Brink said.

The game of Baccarat could be found at most high-end casinos, but the original version of the card game that compared the hands between banker and player was usually relegated to a more elite set of gambling clientele. Brink had picked up an interest in it after seeing Sean Connery play it in some of the early Bond films.

He wasn't a gambler, though. He figured he gambled enough with his own life, so why bother trying to get thrills for a few bucks. Furthermore, if anyone understood long odds, he did. Still, he had taken Jazlyn to a casino or two during their relationship. They had probably lost a hundred dollars all together, but win or lose; they always had a fun time.

"I am surprised you play a game that has the best odds in the casino," Gloria said.

"Having the odds in your favor is always a good thing, Gloria."

"Well, I like to push the envelope myself. The longer the odds, the better the experience. It makes the thrill of victory more powerful. Of all people, I would think you would understand that."

"Sometimes luck runs out."

"And you don't believe in pushing it? Your luck, that is."

"I believe it's time we had a drink," Brink said.

"Lovely, I have been waiting to have a drink with you for a very long time."

Brink addressed the dealer. "My friend, I will have a Madras."

"For the lady?" the dealer asked.

"I will have your best vodka, rocks," she said.

"As you wish."

The dealer started to walk away, but Brink stopped him. "Take your time with the drinks. We need to discuss some sensitive business."

"Of course, sir."

The dealer disappeared and closed the curtain behind him.

"A Madras man," Gloria said. "I wouldn't have expected that."

Brink leaned in closer. "You will find I am full of surprises."

Gloria grabbed his hand. "I want to help you kill them all. They are my enemies as well. I know how to find them. Without me, you will have to strike them directly, but with me at your side we can lure them to their death. They would never expect such treachery from me."

Brink began stroking her hand, moving up to her wrist and forearm. "Is work all you ever think about?" he asked.

Gloria purred. "Hardly," she replied.

She moved in closer, just as the curtain opened, startling her. The dealer returned with a tray of drinks. "Your drinks, sir," he said. He closed the curtain again after setting the tray of drinks down.

They raised their respective glasses, lightly bringing them together, and took a drink. Gloria kept her eyes on the man she desired, and smiled. "Delicious, wouldn't you say? I am referring to the drink, of course."

"Oh yes, I can honestly say that I've never seen a more delicious sight."

At first, Gloria didn't understand. How could this be happening, she asked herself? She felt weak and light headed, as her grasp on the glass began to weaken.

A moment later, her grip on the glass gave out. It fell harmlessly to the carpet below, barely making a sound. She tried to stand up, but her legs were too weak to support her body. Her eyes caught one final image of Aldo Brink casually sipping his drink, just before everything went black.

Brink raised his glass to the dealer and smiled. "You make a mean cocktail, Raj," he said.

Raj bowed his head. "You flatter me, Mr. Brink."

"Is the boat ready?" Brink asked.

"Yes, we can depart anytime."

Brink took another drink and looked down at Gloria. "She should have known, Raj. In the end, the house always wins."

CHAPTER 43

Ben Whitmarsh sat behind his desk, with a half-filled bottle of scotch beside him. His Washington DC law office was immaculate, save for the piles of paperwork segregated in the corner. They were the files related to the Jazlyn Reyes case. He had represented her from the day after the Vice President was killed, and always believed in her innocence.

Things just never added up to the veteran beltway lawyer. Reyes had no motive for premeditated murder, and nothing in her background indicated she had criminal connections, as the government alleged.

The whole thing smacked of a cover up, but he could never get a handle on it. He never got a chance to pull a magic act off in front of the jury due to Jazlyn's escape from prison. Given the long odds he faced in court, perhaps it was for the best when it came to his legal reputation.

Admittedly, he had waivered in his belief of Jazlyn's innocence. The brazen prison break suggested that Jazlyn did have some unsavory friends. Multiple guards were killed in the raid that the news described as one carried out with military precision. How could someone like Jazlyn pull that off? While he had put it in the past, the case still tormented him.

To Ben Whitmarsh, things always needed to make sense. A man killed his wife's lover, or a woman killed her husband for the insurance money, or a man killed the clerk at a convenience store during a robbery. Things like that made sense. Those kinds of cases filled the courts every year, but whatever happened with Jazlyn Reyes didn't fit any criminal template he knew of.

It was late in the evening, but when the phone rang Whitmarsh had a funny feeling it wasn't his wife calling to check up on him. The man on the other end of the phone was the man who hired him to represent Jazlyn as her legal counsel. Whitmarsh knew Aldo Brink as a mild-mannered analyst at the CIA, and Jazlyn's fiancé.

Brink told him that Jazlyn wished to turn herself in. Life on the run had worn heavily on her, and she simply wanted to stop running. He advised Whitmarsh that she would walk into the federal building in the morning, surrender, and plead guilty to all charges. She just wanted it all to be over.

When he hung up the phone, Ben Whitmarsh exhaled. If Jazlyn planned to surrender and plead guilty, then his job was basically done. The judge had suspended the case to allow the authorities some time to locate her, but soon the suspension would be lifted and Jazlyn would be tried and convicted in absentia if she hadn't been found. Now though, the rest of the legal proceedings would be a formality. He could finally put this case behind him, and return to the normal cases that he'd built his career on. Finally, the Jazlyn Reyes case was over.

The next morning Mark Davis perched himself across the street from the federal building where the fugitive Jazlyn Reyes would surrender herself at any moment. He had bugged the phone of her lawyer months ago, but he didn't need a bugged phone to know she would be there. Mark had been tipped off.

The black Accuracy International AW .338 Lapua Magnum rifle laid at the ready. It possessed a five round magazine, but Mark didn't plan on using its full capacity. At this range, with no wind, he would easily put Jazlyn down with one carefully placed shot to the head.

Though his original orders were to leave her alone after the prison escape, Jazlyn had become too big a wild card. Word came down from the highest authority that his orders were changed to take her out. Mark watched with his binoculars as cars rolled by. A little less than an hour into his stakeout, a yellow taxi pulled up in front. Mark zeroed in on it, and reached for his rifle when a woman emerged. Her clothes were a bit shabby, but there Jazlyn Reyes stood, just as his information said.

She wore a long skirt that went down to the ground, and a yellow top. She really stood out. Life on the run had done the once pretty woman no favors, Mark thought. Mark put his eye up to the scope on his rifle and placed the target reticle on her head. He anticipated she would walk towards the door, but he delayed his shot a moment when she didn't move at all. Jazlyn seemed a bit unsteady on her feet. Was she having second thoughts about turning herself in, Mark wondered? He figured that must be it, since he knew he would have the same feelings if he found himself in her shoes. Mark switched the safety on the rifle off.

She started to move gingerly, as Mark put his finger on the trigger. He held his breath, and squeezed it with the dexterity of a skilled marksman. The high powered rifle had a suppressor attached, but the rifle still made a good amount of noise. Luckily, the downtown city noise masked some of it. The bullet screamed through the air on a downward trajectory and struck the fugitive in the head just above her left ear. Mark was already disassembling the rifle and storing it in the hard plastic case he brought with him, when a small crowd gathered around the sidewalk to ghoulishly view the dead body.

After Mark stowed the rifle case in his car, his curiosity got the best of him, and he doubled back to see his handiwork firsthand. When he reached the front of the federal building, the crowd had grown larger and some security officials from inside the building were trying in vain to preserve the crime scene. Onsite Emergency Medical Responders tried to get a pulse, but there was nothing they could do. Before long, an ambulance would arrive to take the body away for an autopsy, closing the case of Jazlyn Reyes forever.

With his work done, Mark started to leave. A second later, out of the corner of his eye, he spotted something that didn't make sense. His eyes had to be playing tricks on him, he thought. He moved closer to the body, and became increasingly aggressive in pushing people out of his way, breaking through the security tape perimeter before a guard stopped him.

By that point he had seen all he needed to though, the unmistakable rose tattoo on his lover Gloria's left ankle, moments before they zipped her dead body into the black zipper bag.

CHAPTER 44

Mark staggered back to his car, waging a futile battle to hide his emotions from the people he passed on the way. How could this have happened, he asked himself? When he got behind the wheel of his vehicle, the answer readily presented itself. A plain white envelope lay taped to the steering wheel. Tearing it open, revealing the grotesque contents inside, he flipped through countless pictures that seemed to show a progression in time.

The first depicted his lover Gloria on what looked to be an operating table. The next had Gloria on the same table, only this time, nude. As he flipped through the photos, he noticed that all of them were taken from an elevated position suggesting some kind of automated camera setup that would snap a photo at whatever time interval the operator set.

The photos told the whole story. Gloria, unconscious on an operating table as a pale bald man in a surgical mask sliced and diced, eventually leaving her with a face that even her lover mistook for Jazlyn Reyes. While it wasn't a perfect match, it was close enough. Only one man could have done this, Mark thought. It had to be Aldo Brink. He kidnapped Gloria and had her face altered, tricking him into killing his own lover. That explained her somewhat hard appearance that Mark attributed to the toll of being on the run. She must have been drugged, which explained her uneven steps upon exiting the taxi.

Mark threw the pictures at the dashboard in frustration. He gripped the steering wheel and squeezed it with all his might, fighting the urge to scream in agony. "That bastard Hodges!" he said to himself.

Brink obviously had been behind Gloria's transformation, but Sam Hodges, the deputy director of the CIA was who ordered Mark Davis to eliminate Jazlyn Reyes in front of the federal building. Mark knew that Brink had called Jazlyn's attorney about turning herself in. He had that phone tapped for months, after all. What he didn't expect was the call he received from Sam Hodges ordering him to put a bullet in her head. He must have been in league with Brink, he thought.

Mark slammed the car into gear and peeled out of the parking garage, leaving a trail of rubber behind. He placed a call to the Deputy Director, who answered immediately.

"I just saw on the news that Jazlyn Reyes was shot outside the federal building" Hodges said.

"Yes. I saw the same thing. We need to meet, now."

"Of course," Hodges said. "You can pick me up at the usual place, and we can discuss our next move."

"I will be there in fifteen."

"See you then. Good work, Mark. I knew I could count on you."

Fifteen minutes later, Mark picked up Hodges and drove through downtown DC. "Is something wrong?" Hodges asked. "You haven't said two words since I got in."

"No, nothing's wrong at all. Just thinking about where we go from here."

"Don't worry. I know Brink is a dangerous man, but we can handle him."

That was the last straw for Mark. This charade had gone on long enough, he thought. He jerked the wheel and parked the car along the side of the road. He reached into his jacket and pulled his pistol. The suppressor made the weapon a little long and awkward for such a small space, but accuracy wouldn't be an issue from this range. He pointed it at the Deputy Director's chest. "You don't think I know what you did!?" Mark screamed.

"What the Hell do you think you're doing? Holster that weapon."

"You bastard. You made me kill her. She was one of us!"

Hodges tensed up. "What are you talking about? Kill who?"

Mark pistol-whipped him across the face. "You had me kill Gloria. Don't deny it."

"Gloria? I ordered you to kill Jazlyn Reyes, you fool, and from the news reports you succeeded."

"Jazlyn isn't dead, but you already know that, you son of a bitch."

"So then who did you shoot?" Hodges asked.

Mark's blood boiled. "Gloria Smith! She was one of our own agents!"

"Why the Hell did you shoot her!?"

This conversation exhausted what little patience Mark had left. He grabbed the white envelope and handed it to his captive. "Open it."

Hodges did as he was told. He flipped through the pictures just as Mark had, becoming more disgusted as he went through them. "Who did this to her?" he asked.

"As if you didn't know," Mark said.

Just as Hodges began to speak, his phone rang. He reached into his jacket.

"Slowly!" Mark shouted. Hodges complied and slowly took his phone out and displayed it to his captor. "Who is it?" Mark asked.

"It says unknown."

"Put it on speaker."

Hodges pressed the speakerphone button, being careful not to make any sudden movements, as Mark looked increasingly unstable. "This is Deputy Director Hodges, who is this?"

"I'm the guy you should've left alone." Aldo Brink had a distinct voice, and the two men recognized it instantly. "You didn't think I knew you tapped her lawyer's phone?"

A thick silence filled the car.

"Nothing to say, boys?" Brink asked.

"How could you do that to Gloria?" Mark asked.

"I got tired of her hitting on me." Brink said.

Silence.

"Yeah, that's right. Your girlfriend couldn't keep her hands off me, but in the end she served a purpose. Now, the whole world will think Jaz is dead."

"You will never be able to keep that story up. There will be an autopsy, DNA…" Hodges said.

"Sam, this is Aldo Brink you're speaking to."

Hodges slumped back in his seat. He understood exactly what the seasoned black ops agent meant. Brink obviously had a plan, and had already worked out all those details.

Brink continued. "Thanks for doing exactly what I knew you would, Sam. I knew you and the Ladies Man would want Jazlyn out of the equation once and for all, and I knew who you would order to do it. That's why I told you she was turning herself in."

Mark put his gun down, understanding he'd kidnapped the wrong man.

"Another thing," Brink said. "If I was able to get into your car and leave an envelope of pictures showing your crazy ass girlfriend's facelift, couldn't I have put something else in, too?"

Mark and Hodges looked at each other with terror apparent on their faces.

"Yeah, that's right, I am sure your diligence was affected by your grief, but whatever you do, don't look straight ahead, it will only make it hurt worse." Naturally, the two men looked forward out the front windshield. They saw Brink talking on a cell phone standing next to a yellow taxi cab with the driver's side door open. "I told ya," he said.

Brink pressed a button on his phone. A second later, Mark Davis and Sam Hodges were engulfed in flames as their car exploded with a force that shook the street. Their dead, but still burning bodies were seen by tens of horrified onlookers. A shopkeeper heroically tried a futile attempt to douse the flames with his garden hose.

Brink casually got back behind the wheel of his yellow taxi, put his seat belt on, and drove away.

CHAPTER 45

Donald Abraham felt guilty. Not about covering up Jazlyn Reyes' faux death, but about how he let her take the fall in the first place. His age had caught up to him, and he knew it. This wouldn't have happened years ago. Then, he would have been strong enough to stop this plot before it started. He would have had the intuition to sniff it out. He didn't know what was being planned behind his back, and that was the only reason why Brink hadn't killed him.

Still, he could have tried to intervene after the fact. Instead, he said nothing as Aldo confronted the President in the Oval Office. The shame he felt overwhelmed him. He was a master at hiding his emotions, but this was too much, even for him. For an instant he was glad his wife had passed away, because he wouldn't have been able to look at her had she been alive given his cowardice during his last days at the CIA.

Lauren had been his loving wife for fifty-one wonderful years. They married young, and never looked back. Children never came, but they always had each other. She supported him during his career the way few women would. He missed Lauren every day since her passing. If she looked down upon him now, he hoped with all his heart that she still loved him despite his terrible inaction.

His last major operation before retiring as the longest serving Director of the CIA would be yet another epic cover-up. Gloria Smith/Volodin would be cremated and all documents would reflect that Jazlyn Reyes died from a gunshot wound to the head; killed by her drug cartel associates who feared her turning state's evidence against them in return for a lighter sentence or better prison accommodations. He owed it to Aldo. That, he knew for sure.

Abraham could only think of one agent he could trust to carry out the cover-up. Brink spared the life of Trent Richards earlier, so he was the natural choice. Trent was a passionate agent, who, when the legendary Director of the CIA asked him to do something, did it. Agent Richards also owed Brink for sparing his life in that parking garage that Sam Hodges sent him into without all the facts.

Agent Richards made sure Gloria's body never got a real examination. False documents were generated to make sure everything looked as it should. Before the medical examiner could even conduct a full autopsy, Richards took the body and cremated it. Juan Reyes gave a tearful statement to the media where he told the world how he and his wife scattered their beloved daughter's ashes in the ocean. Richards was impressed with the performance Juan put on for the media. Brink told him to lay it on thick, and that's just what Jazlyn's father did.

When the medical examiner started asking questions about where the body went, and why he didn't have a chance to examine it, Agent Richards calmly informed him that another doctor did the exam and signed off on the report. When the medical examiner persisted, Richards made it clear that the man's career and his family's security would be in jeopardy if he didn't drop it. Everyone was ready to move on, and conspiracy theories wouldn't be tolerated, Richards told him. Just as Mark Davis had staged a mugging to hide the murder of the original Thornburg pathologist, Richards was more than capable of doing the same thing to this medical examiner. Richards didn't think it would need to get that far.

There would be some nagging questions from the FBI, Congress, and the media, but in the end there was no proof of anything other than the official story. There was no body to examine, and the DNA records provided showed a match to Jazlyn Reyes. The White House swallowed the tall tale, hook, line, and sinker. They wanted to move on and were happy to see Jazlyn Reyes dead and out of their hair.

Abraham had finally done the right thing. Still, many innocent people had suffered and died, in part due to his cowardice. As he took a final drink for the night, he reflected on his years of service. He served his country since the age of 18, first in the military, and then in the CIA.

His final act was as close to a high note as he ever had while in the big chair. Better late than never, he supposed.

CHAPTER 46

The mask fit snugly. As the van approached its destination, Aldo Brink adjusted it one last time. The yellow skull mask provided no additional protection, but it did provide him an edge in battle. Brink always utilized the element of surprise whenever possible, and when his targets saw a hulking figure dressed in black, blazing away with a yellow skull head, they naturally flinched. Sometimes, this flinch meant the difference between life and death.

Brink and the Harrison brothers were on their way to a party. Naturally they dressed for the occasion. Tactical black clothing from head to toe with ballistic armor might not be normal attire for a night out at the club, but tonight it suited the three of them just fine.

Rodney Harrison strolled through the deserted side alley next to the private club of Anton Volodin. At 3 AM the streets were empty. The only activity in the area would be found inside the club. The Russian Mafia kingpin and

GRU operative had a routine. Unfortunately for him, Brink and the Harrison brothers knew it backwards and forwards. Once a month, he would call in his entire crew to discuss business, drink, and ogle the countless prostitutes who were in attendance.

Volodin had been marginally useful to Brink, but when he decided to kidnap Jazlyn and use her as a suicide bomber against the President, his usefulness plummeted to zero.

"Side door secure," Rodney said into his Bluetooth earpiece.

"Back door in position," Brink replied.

"Waiting on big brother," Hakim said.

After completing his task, Rodney rounded the corner and approached the front door. Upon seeing his older brother, Hakim did the same from the opposite side. They would reach the front door together in ten seconds where a lone Russian sentry stood smoking a cigarette. Security wasn't tight as no one would ever dare attack Anton Volodin in his own club. The local Atlantic City hoods knew to stay away.

Sadly for the sentry, the trench coat wearing Harrison Brothers were anything but local hoods. The Russian had just finished stepping on his cigarette butt, when he looked up and saw a hulking man in a black trench coat wearing a black ski mask mere feet from him. In a panic, he reached for his pistol. Hakim snapped his neck from behind before he could even draw it, and then carried him inside the front door as Rodney followed. Once inside, they checked the entryway, and secured the front door from the inside with a thick steel chain and lock. After shedding their trench coats, they moved to the double doors that lead to the main hall.

"Party crashers in position," Hakim said. "We go on you."

In the back alley, Brink had already dispatched the Russian standing guard. After shooting him in the head with a suppressed subsonic hollow point round, he promptly picked the man up and dropped him into a nearby dumpster. Brink entered the building and secured the rear door with a thick steel chain and lock from the inside.

He moved forward to the door leading to the main hall. Quickly, he removed the fiber optic camera from the pouch on his belt and slid it under the door. The image on the small LCD screen showed Anton Volodin and his group of henchman drinking and laughing the night away.

"Girls have been moved out," Brink said.

"Copy that."

Brink and the Harrison Brothers were about to turn Anton Volodin's club into a shooting gallery. The prostitutes getting caught in the cross fire was something they wanted to avoid, but Brink knew that if one got in between him and the Russian kingpin, he wouldn't hesitate.

They knew that after a while Volodin had his goons herd the ladies into a room while he discussed more sensitive matters with his men. Rodney had been keeping tabs on the place for some time and had the schedule down to the minute. Just like at the prison, Rodney's timing was perfect.

After stowing the camera in his pouch, Brink readied his weapons. He had a surprise for the Russians courtesy of Taylor Ross, the loyal technology specialist who had backed him up time after time. As he held the same M249 PARA that he used when he assaulted the prison, he spoke decisively.

"Party crashers… Execute."

Anton Volodin sat in his favorite lounge chair, a cigar in one hand, and a whiskey on the rocks in the other. His deep laugh bellowed through the room as he watched his men get lap dances by the scantily clad women he hired for the evening. The chair to his right, normally filled with the burly Nikolai Kozlov, was empty.

He said goodbye to his top henchman as he boarded a plane back to Russia. There he could have specialists fit him with a prosthetic in place of the hand that Aldo Brink took from him. Going to American doctors was out of the question, as it would mean too many questions and inevitable interference from the authorities. They would have their revenge, but it would happen at a time of their choosing. They would hunt Aldo Brink down like a dog, and torture him to death.

"Move them out," Volodin said.

A bald Russian nodded his head, and ushered the girls away. As the girls were herded into an adjacent soundproof room, a younger Russian sat down in the chair usually occupied by Nikolai. Volodin stared at the young GRU agent, who seemed oblivious to his misstep.

"Get out of that chair!" Volodin barked. "You will sit on the floor like the dog you are."

The young Russian sheepishly withdrew from the chair, and bowed his head, begging for forgiveness from the dangerous gangster. "Forgive me," he said.

"Just sit on the floor, dog." Fearing Volodin's wrath, the young man complied.

Now that the girls had been locked in an adjacent lounge room, Volodin could get down to business before bringing them back to satisfy his men. He held court like a sage wizard who had seen it all. Some sat in luxurious chairs, some at the bar, and some even stood to listen to the legendary GRU operative and Mafioso.

The young Russian tried to rise from the floor but was immediately pushed back down by the same bald man who had wrangled the ladies moments earlier.

"Soon comrades we will strike a fatal blow," Volodin said. "Even now, my daughter provides us critical information about the enemy from the inside. Her dedication to our cause should be a model for you all."

The men raised their glasses to Gloria in salute. After her father gave the signal, they drank and gave a cheer.

"But all things are not perfect, comrades. The dog, Aldo Brink, has killed our brothers in Miami! Promise me that you will find him, and bring him to me!"

Volodin's lust for vengeance echoed through the main hall. Before he could continue his diatribe, the doors at the front and rear of the hall burst open.

Even though he needed to wait for the go order from Aldo, Hakim entered the main hall first. He had been itching for some action since the day that Aldo explained what happened to Jazlyn. Hakim wanted blood and that's exactly what he found when he stormed into the main hall.

Brink entered from the rear, while the Harrison brothers stormed in through the front. Hakim unloaded on the first Russian he saw with his own M249. The Russians were in various states of drunkenness and in no condition to fight, but in this case it wouldn't have mattered.

Half tried in vain to draw their pistols and return fire. Those courageous souls were cut to ribbons by the Harrison brothers. They each covered half the room as they spread out and flanked inward from where they came in. The other half, startled by two huge men wearing ski masks who shot first without asking any questions, panicked and ran to the back of the hall hoping to escape.

They were met with a chained door and a terrifying man in a yellow skull mask who gunned them down four at a time. Back in the main hall, the Russians had been decimated. Only the young Russian who Volodin had disciplined and Volodin himself remained alive. The brothers followed Brink's strict orders that Volodin was to remain breathing. The young Russian survived simply by lying flat on the ground and not moving, perhaps saved by his floor seat courtesy of his boss.

In a desperate act of bravado, the fat old Russian lunged for a dead man's pistol, but was met with the massive boot of Hakim Harrison that struck him across the face. Volodin saw stars for a few moments.

"Stay on the ground where you belong, you fat ass pig!" Hakim howled.

The young Russian trembled. "Don't worry, kid," Rodney said. "You will make it through this as long as you don't do anything stupid. We want you to go back and tell them what you saw here."

Volodin, not content to stay put, gestured to the young one. "Do something, you coward!" he screamed.

The young Russian reached for a pistol that lay on the ground. "Don't do it," Rodney warned.

The second he touched it, Hakim shot him in the chest several times. He slumped over, and fell to the ground. "Bastards," Volodin said. "You will pay for this!"

Brink, still masked, walked into the main hall. "I've heard that before," he said.

"Who are you?" Volodin asked.

Brink pulled off his mask, and unzipped a pocket on his vest. "I'm the mailman." Brink pulled a stack of pictures from his pocket and tossed them to Volodin.

As the grizzled Russian looked at them, he reacted just as Mark Davis did. He had seen on the news that Jazlyn Reyes was killed, and had taken great joy in that. Now, he saw that the news had been a lie. Even worse, his own daughter Gloria had been butchered and now lay dead.

"Don't be too sad, Anton," Brink said. "She was double crossing you the whole time. In fact, she wanted me to help her kill you for everything you put her through as a child…She hated you, Anton."

Volodin slumped over and tossed the pictures aside, resigned to his fate. "Shoot me and get it over with, you dog!"

"Not so fast. This is courtesy of my friend Taylor." Brink flipped a switch on the left side of his belt. Attached to the switch was a small compressed gas tank enclosed by bullet resistant Kevlar. The tank had a Kevlar coated hose that ran up his back, over his shoulder, and down his arm to his wrist. Brink held his arm out, as the Harrison brothers quickly moved out of the way.

With a flick of his wrist, a stream of fire erupted from the device in his hand and shot six feet across the room. Volodin ignited even easier than Brink thought he would, but realized he had been covered in Russian alcohol during the chaos of the shootout which added to his combustibility. Volodin screamed in terror and lunged throughout the room trying desperately to put the fire out. As the stink of his burning flesh filled the room, Brink put him out of his misery and emptied the rest of his M249 rounds into the screaming man.

Hakim took his mask off, looking disappointed. "What's wrong?" Brink asked.

"That would have been better if we had witnesses to see it," he said.

"Well, don't kill them all next time."

Hakim nodded in acceptance.

The three men walked together to the side door that Rodney chained from the outside to prevent escape. It lead to the van parked in the side alley. They would be gone long before the police arrived. The building had been constructed with soundproofing in mind, so there stood a good chance no one outside even heard the commotion. Just as Rodney was about to blow the door open with a small explosive charge, he stopped.

"Aldo, should we do anything about the girls locked in that room?"

He thought about it for moment. "We should do what any concerned citizen would do," Brink said. "Call the police."

Rodney blew the door. Within seconds the three men were driving away, as the elder Harrison brother made a polite call to 911 to report a commotion, and some scantily clad women in the neighborhood.

CHAPTER 47

Jazlyn looked beautiful. She suffered some minor burns on her face from the explosion that Soham's doctor equated to what happens to your hand when you accidentally grab a hot pan from the stove. Raj's special oil combined with the cream the doctor prescribed did the trick. The redness had completely faded, and she looked as good as new. Brink had sold the "distraught man grieving over his horribly disfigured fiancée" quite well to Gloria over the phone.

Her knee had been the real concern. It required surgery after the fall she took. As always, Soham assured Aldo his doctor would ask no questions and would forget everything the second the surgery was over. To the doctor, it was just a routine procedure for a friend of his most important patient anyway. Doing a quick favor for Soham Gupta, who paid twice the normal rate, was a no brainer, and the doctor was happy to help. Jazlyn used a fake name, just to be sure though.

Jazlyn rested comfortably in her bed at Soham's estate. When Aldo walked in, her smile returned.

"Are you in any pain?" asked Brink.

"No. It's just a little stiff."

Brink sat down on the bed next to her. "The doctor said it would be stiff for a little while, but after some physical therapy, you will be running with me in the morning like old times."

"If you say it, I believe it."

Brink smiled. "So, anything exciting been going on lately?"

Jazlyn burst out laughing. In that moment they both realized that she hadn't laughed in months. With everything going on, it wasn't surprising. She couldn't help but wonder what would happen next. Would they be on the run forever? Could they even have a life? After her laughter subsided, she broached the question.

"Aldo, what happens now?" she asked.

"We settle down, get married, and have a wonderful life together. I already resigned from the agency. I spoke to the Director himself. He wishes us the best."

"That easy, huh?"

"That easy."

"How? I am a fugitive and awful people are trying to kill us."

"No one will ever look for you again," Brink said. "I took care of it."

Raj, Soham's loyal butler, walked in with a tray of food and an American newspaper. "Good afternoon, I have some lunch for you," he said.

Brink snatched the newspaper and showed Jazlyn the front page.

"Congratulations on your death, Miss Jazlyn," Raj said. "I am sure it gives you great relief."

Jazlyn understood when she saw the front page.

Jazlyn Reyes Killed By Drug Cartel

She scanned down and read the cover story that accompanied it. So that's why no one would be coming after me anymore, she thought.

"Aldo, what is this?" she asked.

"I faked your death. No one will ever come looking for you again. You will have to use a fake identity like we talked about, and keeping your hair a different color is a wise precaution, but you are free. We will practice using the fake identity, so you don't get tripped up while out in public if someone asks you any questions."

Jazlyn felt grateful, but also thought of something terrible. Her parents would also think she was dead and would read how she was involved with drugs and evil people. "What about my parents?" she asked.

"I made contact with them. They know you're alive. They're happy you can have a life now. They don't care what others think. They know the truth, and that's all that matters to them."

"So, I can see them again?"

"Absolutely. Once we get settled and I know things are safe, they will come and visit. They are eager to see our wedding."

"Oh, Aldo."

"I know you wanted a big wedding with your whole family, but it will have to be quite a bit smaller, for safety's sake."

"As long as I have you, everything will be fine."

"May I attend, Mr. Brink?" Raj asked.

Jazlyn extended her hand to the loyal butler. He took it and placed his other had on top. "I would be honored if you came," she said.

"I will be there. Good luck, Miss Jazlyn." Raj turned and left the room, closing the door behind him.

Brink took her hand. "Jaz, there is still one more thing I have to do before we can get on with our lives together. It will only take a few days."

"What is it?"

"The President thinks you are dead, but I have to speak with him."

"Oh my God, Aldo. What are you going to do?"

"Let him know that I know what he did. He didn't know the details, but he ordered Sam Hodges to frame an innocent person for the death of the Vice President. It went sideways, because he had no idea it would be you, but his craven nature started everything."

Jazlyn sat up. "Aldo, I want you to listen to me. We are free now. You don't have to go back there and do whatever it is you're going to do. Please, don't go."

"I have to, Jaz."

"Let it go," she said.

Those words echoed in Brink's mind. They were the same words he spoke to Sam Hodges, warning the Deputy Director not to pursue him. Maybe he needed to leave well enough alone this time, and take Jazlyn's advice.

He thought about it for a few seconds, kissed Jazlyn on the head, and reached his decision.

CHAPTER 48

The grand ballroom had the stench of politics. The key swing state of Florida hosted tonight's event at one of the trendiest hotels in Ft. Lauderdale. Over the years, President Richard Wilson had worked countless rooms just like this. They all looked the same. The CEOs, lawyers, lobbyists, and every special interest group imaginable always found a way to snag a seat at these Presidential functions, and the President loved to glad hand them.

There were a few politicians in America who truly didn't have big egos, but Richard Wilson wasn't one of them. He basked in the adulation, even if it came from media sycophants and yes men. "Welcome to Florida, Mr. President!" a man shouted as a sea of hands extended to touch the most powerful man on Earth.

"It's always great to be in the Sunshine State!" Wilson shouted.

The service staff buzzed around the floor with trays of fattening appetizers and glasses of champagne. Soon, the President would give a speech to his adoring fans. Afterwards, he would sit down to eat a twenty five thousand dollar per plate fish dinner with his wealthier ones. For now, the Commander in Chief was content to mingle with the attendees, while his rat-like Chief of Staff whispered relevant information into his ear.

After a while, the immediate crowd had thinned, and the President found himself engaging in smaller, more in-depth conversations. Most involved his big money financial donors, the most important group at any Presidential event. A waiter arrived with a tray of drink orders, but the President hastily brushed him off despite the fact that the donors he was speaking to had ordered them.

"Sir," the waiter interrupted. "I believe they ordered these."

The President sheepishly motioned for the drinks. "I'm sorry. I was caught up telling a story," he said.

"No problem at all, Mr. President." The donors took their drinks and thanked the waiter for bringing them.

"You lived in Florida long?" the President asked the server.

"All my life," the waiter said.

"Wonderful. It's hard-working people like you who make this country great."

Even the donors chuckled a little when he uncorked that line of political bullshit. The waiter politely nodded and smiled, causing his large mustache to curl upwards which caught the President's attention. "I love your mustache. I had one years ago, but the wife didn't like it," he said. The waiter nodded and politely excused himself.

Chris Spencer, the head of the President's Secret Service protection detail, stood watch. He didn't have to be there, but he loved standing a post. Tonight, he had no official post, but simply operated as a free agent. He scanned the crowd with eyes of steel. A clean cut waiter approached, and handed him a note. "Sir, one of your agents asked me to give you this," he said.

"What agent?" Spencer asked.

"Oh, I don't know. I wasn't paying attention, really."

Without even looking at the note, Spencer knew something was wrong. No agent of his would pass a note to him through a waiter. They had secure radios and would never trust a civilian with any information. "Think. What did he look like?"

"Well, he was white, with darker hair. I guess that's it."

Spencer dismissed the man and unfolded the piece of paper. The note was short and to the point.

I'm here. BRINK.

"Spencer to Torque. Check in. We have an intruder."

CHAPTER 49

Torque was the code word for the agents on the President's security detail. As Spencer worked his way through the crowd towards the President, a sense of relief came over him as all the designated agents checked in and reported nothing unusual.

He interrupted the President in mid-sentence as he spoke to an attractive woman. "Excuse me sir, I need to speak with you, now."

"What on Earth is it?"

"Sir, in private."

"Very well." The president took Spencer by the arm and moved away. "What is it?"

"Mr. President, we need to get you out of here now. I don't want to cause a panic or make you look bad by rushing you out, but you need to go."

"Why? You must have some reason. If there was an imminent threat you would already be shuffling me out against my will."

Spencer handed him the note. The President read it and handed it back to him. "This could very well be an idle threat. You have no proof he is here or that anything is wrong, do you?"

"No, sir."

"Well, then I trust you and your men will protect me. Chris, every event I go to there are notes like this and we don't shut them down. Your men are covering the whole event. How could he even get in?"

"He's Aldo Brink. That's what he does," Spencer said.

The President's chief of staff interrupted. "Sir, it's time."

"Take whatever actions you need to, but I am giving this speech. These people are funding my campaign!" Wilson barked.

With that, the President walked on stage to cheers and the adulation he so coveted. After a few minutes of speaking, Spencer relaxed a little. His awareness remained high, but with each passing minute, his sense of dread lifted. The feeling didn't last long when an agent failed to respond during check in.

"Torque to Spencer, Agent Reynolds is down. I repeat Agent Reynolds is down!" The voice over his earpiece made his heart sink. Seconds later, another terrified voice came over it. "Agent Baker is down. We have no twenty on the intruder!"

"Oh my God," Spencer said to himself. "How can this be happening?"

Instinct kicked in. It wasn't an idle threat. Brink was here, and Spencer needed to get the President out of there. As he walked up the side stairs of the stage, panic gripped the Grand Ballroom.

Thick white smoke poured out of the ventilation ducts into the hall. A woman yelled "Fire!" and another man shouted that it was a terrorist attack. Others started to cough as chaos erupted. People shoved each other to the ground while trying to escape the room, fearful of breathing the toxic gas.

By the time Spencer reached the podium, another agent had already grabbed the President. They ushered him off the stage with other agents through a side door. The designated escape route was through several long hallways, down to the kitchen, and out through the service door where the Presidential limo awaited.

An agent reported in to Spencer through his earpiece.

"Stagecoach in position."

While Presidents had different codenames, his limo always went by "Stagecoach." Once they got him to it, the President would be fine. It would practically take a tank to put a dent in the thing.

They traversed the long hallway with great haste as the agents pushed the President along faster than he wanted to go. When they reached the kitchen, another agent reported in to Spencer. "Sir, there is no threat in the ballroom. No threat! There were several smoke machines like you'd see in a haunted house."

Spencer felt relieved that no one was dead up in the ballroom, but the report changed nothing. He was getting the President out of there, now. Still, why smoke machines, he wondered?

As they approached the utility service area, it all started to make sense to him. Just then, the ceiling shook, the walls trembled, and everything went black.

CHAPTER 50

They were trapped. Their route had been closed off by explosive charges. Two explosions, one in front, and one in the rear had resulted in concrete and steel caving them in. Spencer and the three other agents surrounded the President in a last ditch effort to protect him from falling debris, or whatever else lurked in the darkness.

Spencer had walked right into Aldo Brink's trap, and he knew it. The note was the first bread crumb, and if that hadn't forced him to evacuate the President, the smoke and panic would have for sure. He tried to get ahold of someone on his radio, but the concrete blocked all radio signals. He thought of trying to dig out one stone at a time, but that risked collapsing the whole tunnel, he thought. No, they would have to wait to be rescued.

Before they had a chance to catch their breath, a smaller explosion caved in the wall to their left. The dust and smoke burned as it filled their lungs. Emerging from the hole in the wall was Chris Spencer's worst nightmare. He feared this day would come from the moment Aldo told him what happened to Jazlyn, his fiancée.

Due to the lack of light, the yellow skull was the only thing the five men saw. Brink expanded a collapsible baton as he approached the agents. By the time they regained their senses from the smaller blast, two were already knocked unconscious, while the third hopelessly tried to draw his gun. Brink spun the man around, snapped his arm at the elbow, and knocked him out cold with a baton strike to the head.

Spencer put his body in front of the President, and aimed his weapon straight ahead. His eyes burned from the dust and smoke. His breathing picked up, but his hands remained steady as he tried to find his target. From the darkness, a baton strike whipped through the air, knocking the gun out of his strong hands. Brink hit him again, and again, but not hard enough to knock him out. Brink picked up the gun, unloaded it and dismantled it within seconds flinging the parts back into the darkness.

He moved toward the shivering President, cracking him once in the head with the baton before retracting it and returning it to his belt.

"What do you want!?" the President screamed. "I will give you anything you want! I am Richard Wilson, the President of the United States! Do you hear me?"

Brink grabbed him by the throat with his right hand, lifted him off his feet, and held him against the cold concrete wall. With his left hand, he removed the skull mask and stuffed it in his pouch. "I want Jazlyn back," Brink said.

Brink relaxed his grip slightly allowing Wilson to speak. "I didn't know it was going to be her! You have to believe me."

"You put it all in motion, and now she is dead. If it were up to me, you would be dead too. The last thing she said to me before she tried to turn herself in was that I needed to let it go. She begged me not to kill you."

Spencer started to get up, but Brink put an end to that with a kick to his ribs with his left foot. Spencer slammed back into the wall, clutching his midsection.

"You see, Dick," Brink said. "Jazlyn showed mercy on you. You destroyed her life, and she still took mercy on you and begged me not to kill you. That is the only reason you are still alive. I am honoring her dying wish. You need to thank her for that. Say thank you, Jazlyn."

The President looked bewildered. "Say it!" Brink demanded.

"Thank you, Jazlyn," Wilson said with a whimper.

Brink dropped the President and pushed him against the wall next to Spencer. He drew his HK45 and pointed it at the President's head.

"Aldo, no! Don't do it," Spencer pleaded.

"Chris, we were wrong all these years. We do have a choice in who we protect," Brink said. "I'm letting it go. You both better do the same. Blame this on a terrorist attack where you were saved by heroic Secret Service agents. If you send anyone after me or do anything other than drop it completely, I will come back here. And when I do, I'll kill all you sons of bitches."

Brink cracked them each one more time in the head, knocking them out. He turned, and disappeared into the darkness.

EPILOGUE

To Aldo Brink, the calm waters of Lake Como made sense. The violent storm that he and Jazlyn endured had finally passed. While their engagement had been tumultuous to say the least, their wedding would be serene. He and Jazlyn stayed on the move, splitting time between a few properties that Aldo discreetly purchased. Jazlyn always wanted to honeymoon in Italy, so Brink did one better and bought a charming villa right on Lake Como. It would not only serve as one of their homes, but also as the site of their wedding ceremony.

Brink hadn't picked up any sign of trouble the past few months. Save for a few people, the whole world thought Jazlyn was dead, and Aldo himself had never been charged with a crime. Donald Abraham would retire soon and all his secrets would die with him. He promoted Trent Richards to Deputy Director, replacing the departed Sam

Hodges and groomed him as his successor. Abraham had enough dirt on everyone in Washington to bury the place twice over and gave this information to his new deputy, so when Abraham retired, Richards would carry on the secret of Jazlyn Reyes forever.

If President Richard Wilson had any doubts about who died in front of that federal building, they were laid to rest when Brink put on an award winning caliber performance in the collapsed tunnel. He played the grieving fiancé quite well. He didn't think Wilson would send anyone after him. After all, there was nothing in it for him, and the risk reward ratio made no sense.

Ironically, Jazlyn had saved the President's life, just not exactly in the way Brink said. He let it go, just like she asked him to. For Brink, that meant not killing him and moving on.

Standing by the water, in their backyard, Brink waited as Jazlyn walked down the aisle towards him. In attendance were her parents, who made the trip with some help from Aldo and Soham Gupta. They made sure they weren't followed or tracked in any way.

Her father, Juan, walked Jazlyn down the aisle, and beamed with pride while her mother looked on from the first row of chairs. Soham's daughter Priyanka served as Jazlyn's maid of honor. Soham made the trip as well and took great pains not to be spotted. His fame in his home country made it difficult to come and go without being noticed, but he made it work. Raj, the loyal butler, performed the duties of the best man with charm and class.

Everyone in attendance would die before revealing the truth about Jazlyn's "death." They all owed Aldo Brink their lives in one way or another, and their loyalty was unquestioned.

The final two attendees were, of course, the Harrison brothers. Rodney dressed to the nines as always in a dark suit, while Hakim wore a white one, with a top hat that struggled to contain his hair. The younger brother also augmented his outfit with a spiffy cane. Hakim always loved a good party, and that evening's reception was right up his alley. At the party, he would pick Jazlyn up, spin her around, and ask her a question.

"Do you have a sister?" Alas, she was an only child.

When Jazlyn reached him, Aldo couldn't stop smiling. Everything had been worth it, he thought. As the priest began the ceremony, Aldo knew everything would be fine, with fine being a relative term. They would never be a normal couple, but they would strive for it anyway.

Aldo could still use his name for many things, but Jazlyn would forever have to use another, including at their own wedding for the sake of the priest, the only person in attendance unaware of the circumstances that the happy couple faced. He also knew even with all his precautions, danger could lurk around any corner.

No matter though, I have a plan, and I will always be ready.

ABOUT THE AUTHOR

Dan Chakonas is an avid reader and student of literature. His love for books began after reading <u>Treasure Island</u> by Robert Louis Stevenson. The adventure and unique characters inspired him to embark on a journey of creating his own literary heroes and villains.

He holds a bachelor's degree in English from Northeastern Illinois University. He lives in the Chicago area and enjoys its great museums, restaurants, and sports.

BRINK is Dan's first novel.

SOLITUDE BOOKS

Please visit Solitude Books online to order and to see future exciting titles!

Aldo Brink will return!

www.solitudebooks.com